'[Kadare] captures the paranoid nature of life under constant surveillance . . . and produces an ironic masterpiece'

Daily Mail

'Melodrama, tragedy and myth illuminate the relationship between individual and state in a fine novel from the great Albanian writer'

Guardian

'A compelling amalgam of realism, dreaminess and elegiac, white-hot fury'

Financial Times

'The literature Kadare has produced in the face of obstacles lesser writers would find insuperable, is, genuinely, of world significance'

The Times

'Coolly ironic writing, which traverses ominous themes of censorship and state control'

Daily Telegraph

'Kadare is a master at braiding narrative strands . . . *A Girl in Exile* is one of Kadare's best novels, and essential reading for our morally uneasy times'

Times Literary Supplement

ISMAIL KADARE

Ismail Kadare is Albania's best-known novelist and poet. Translations of his novels have appeared in more than forty countries. He was awarded the inaugural Man Booker International Prize in 2005 and the Jerusalem Prize in 2015.

John Hodgson studied at Cambridge and Newcastle and has taught at the universities of Prishtina and Tirana. This is the fourth novel by Ismail Kadare that he has translated.

ISMAIL KADARE

A Girl in Exile

Requiem for Linda B.

TRANSLATED FROM THE ALBANIAN BY
John Hodgson

VINTAGE

*Dedicated to the young Albanian women who were born, grew up
and spent their youth in internal exile.*

1 3 5 7 9 10 8 6 4 2

Vintage
20 Vauxhall Bridge Road,
London SW1V 2SA

Vintage is part of the Penguin Random House group of companies
whose addresses can be found at global.penguinrandomhouse.com

This book has been selected to receive financial assistance from
English PEN's "PEN Translates!" programme, supported by Arts
Council England. English PEN exists to promote literature and our
understanding of it, to uphold writers' freedoms around the world,
to campaign against the persecution and imprisonment of writers
for stating their views, and to promote the friendly co-operation of
writers and the free exchange of ideas www.englishpen.org

First published in Vintage in 2017
First published in Great Britain by Harvill Secker in 2016
First published with the title *E penguara: Requiem për Linda B.* in
Albania by Onufri in 2009

www.vintage-books.co.uk

A CIP catalogue record for this book is available from the British Library

ISBN 9780099593072

Printed and bound in Great Britain by Clays Ltd, St Ives PLC

Penguin Random House is committed to a sustainable future for our
business, our readers and our planet. This book is made from Forest
Stewardship Council® certified paper.

I

U NTIL HE reached the end of Dibra Street, it seemed
to him that he had succeeded in thinking of nothing
at all. But when he found himself next to the Tirana Hotel
on the north side of Skanderbeg Square, he felt a sense of
urgency, even panic. Only this square lay between him and
the Party Committee building. Now he could no longer
pretend to be more composed than he was, or reassure
himself with the thought that his conscience was clear. He
had only to cross this square, and however huge it might
be, it was too short a distance for anyone who had been
summoned to the Party Committee without explanation.

With frenzied repetition, as if this were the only way
he could make up for lost time, he rehearsed the two possible issues that might, unknown to him, have got him
into trouble: his latest play, which he had been waiting two
weeks for permission to stage, and his relationship with
Migena.

At any other time the second matter would have worried him more than the first. As he drew near the National Bank, the final scene of their quarrel replayed itself in
his mind with excruciating clarity. The setting had been

the same as that of their previous spat: the corner in his apartment where his bookshelves met the window. They had exchanged almost the same words and her tears had been the same. In fact it was the tears that had scared him. Without them he might have broken off their relationship two weeks earlier. He would have taken her for an over-excited girl from the Art College, who herself didn't know what she wanted. Every time she wept he hoped to find out what her tears concealed, if anything. He had been sure that this was his last chance. 'What's the matter?' he had asked hoarsely. 'At least tell me.' 'I can't. I don't know myself,' she replied. 'You don't know yourself? Really? You think you're so complicated? With all those Marlene Dietrich messages – I love you, I don't love you? Is that what it's all about?'

He felt she was not in control of herself. 'Listen, you're not complicated at all. You're only . . .' An airhead from the provinces, he wanted to say, but restrained himself. 'You're just schizophrenic, or a spy . . .'

He bit his tongue, but the word was out.

'No,' she replied, yet less sharply than he'd expected. 'I'm neither of those things.'

'Then out with it. What the hell's got into you? Tell me, and don't keep saying you don't know.'

He had stretched out his hand as if to seize a girl by the hair two or three times in his life, but he had never actually done it. Now it happened with unexpected ease. He thought his grip would loosen at once and he would let go of those strands as if they were flames, but his hand did not obey him and angrily he pushed that lovely head, which he had caressed so sweetly only a short time ago, against the bookshelves. A comb fell, and after the comb a pile of books whose names for some reason forced themselves up onto his frantic eyes: Scott Fitzgerald, *Toponyms of Albania and Kosovo*, Plutarch.

It was a mere forty seconds to the door of the Party Committee, but enough time for him to realise that, if she had reported him, he couldn't care less. In fact he would prefer a denunciation by her, even with the word 'spy' in it, to any hitch to his play.

He chided himself as a hopeless idiot, unable to see how dangerous a denunciation could be. But this denunciation not only failed to worry him, it seemed to him that he secretly desired it.

As he crossed the threshold of the main entrance, he understood the reason why: he hoped that, whatever trouble it caused him, it might bring its own consolation, as they say every evil does. It might enable him to fathom something that had tortured him now for weeks – the enigma of that girl.

The U-shaped table was familiar to him, but this was the first time that he had sat down alone on its right-hand side. The second secretary and an unknown man had taken their places at the section that connected the two arms of the U. What was this summons about? Why no prior explanation? There was no question of a glass of water or a coffee, but they might at least have said, We're sorry to trouble you, or asked irritating, vapid questions, like: How's the creative process?

He braced himself against the chair back, bristling with the obscure sort of anger that at least helps you keep your dignity, as his friend Llukan Herri would say.

As if reading his mind, the second secretary spoke without preamble and said that the Party valued his work for the stage. This was why the Party Committee had summoned him here to explain a matter for which other people would have had to answer to the Investigator's Office. Before the second secretary had finished speaking, he turned his head towards the stranger, who could be supposed to have come from that office. The investigator's expression was calm, almost benign.

'We require an explanation, or rather two or three simple explanations,' the investigator said, looking down at some sheets of paper in front of him. 'I think you will help us.'

'Of course,' he replied. It must be Act Two, he thought, where the ghost appears. He had noticed that any slip-ups generally happened at the end of Act Two. But still he didn't understand why he should answer for this to an investigator rather than to the theatre's Artistic Board, as was usual.

'It's a sensitive issue,' the investigator continued.

'I still don't see why I have to explain it here.'

The two officials looked at each other.

'Comrade,' said the second secretary. 'I explained to you that this is because of the Party's respect for you. If you would prefer the Investigator's Office . . .'

The investigator bit his lip and made an unintelligible gesture with his hand. He was clearly uneasy.

The Investigator's Office, he wondered. Had it gone that far? 'I'm listening,' he said.

The investigator studied his notes.

'It's a matter of a young girl,' he said, calmly and very slowly.

Aha, he thought. So it is the other thing. Not the auditorium with the red velvet seats, the silence of the audience before the prolonged applause and the shouts of 'Author, author.' They weren't the problem. It was the girl. As if suddenly illuminated by lightning he saw the cleft between her breasts and then her incomprehensible tears.

Maybe she'd known that something was wrong, he thought with a twinge. That it would turn out badly.

'So, do you know this girl?' the investigator asked, and said something else, perhaps her name, but in his confusion the playwright couldn't concentrate. How had she foreseen this blow while he hadn't? he thought to himself reproachfully.

'So you do know her,' the investigator continued, leafing through the file.

He nodded, and tried to summon up his anger, which for some reason was now subsiding. So what? Where was the crime? At one time, affairs of this kind were punishable, especially when they involved well-known people who were supposed to set a moral example, but nobody paid any attention to them anymore. Only when there were scandals, broken families, or connections to the former bourgeoisie. Or when the girl herself made a complaint.

Why might Migena have lodged a complaint? He thought of his brutal behaviour by the bookshelves, and the word 'spy' that had no doubt incensed her more than anything else. Did you use the word 'spy' or not? We'd like to know in what sense. A spy for whom, against whom? You know that our state does not use spies . . . Why had he used that bloody word? He hadn't been asked about it yet but he had his answer ready. He hadn't meant it in a political sense. He had said it in a flash of anger, as it's used in daily life about people with loose tongues.

'I'm sure you won't take offence if I ask you about the nature of your relationship,' the investigator said.

'Of course not,' the playwright replied, relieved that the girl had not maligned him. 'I've nothing to hide. It was, or rather is, a love relationship – what you would call intimate.'

'Really?' the investigator replied. 'So a love affair, with dates and all the rest of it . . .'

'Yes,' said the playwright.

The second secretary and the investigator looked at each other in clear astonishment.

'Is there anything hard to believe here?' the playwright said. 'If I'd denied it, as people often do, and had said I didn't know her, had never seen her and so on, you'd have every right to be suspicious. But I'm not hiding anything. I admit we were having an affair. A love affair, you called it. Where's the harm?'

Still they stared at him.

'I mean, is this really serious enough to make a case out of it?'

He wanted to add that of course it was nothing to boast about, when the thought of Albana struck him like a lightning bolt. My God, he thought, how could he have forgotten her? How could she have vanished from his mind that morning, when he should have been thinking especially of her?

'Perhaps you know,' he said hesitantly, 'I . . .'

Perhaps they did know, there was no way they couldn't, that for some time he had been living with a doctor, whom he would certainly have married that summer if she had not gone to Austria on a four-month internship. To study sedatives. 'Anaesthetics' was the medical term. Perhaps he was now adding unnecessary details, burbling nonsense that was of no use to anybody. But perhaps it did provide an explanation. In cases like this, a woman's long absence could cause complications.

It wasn't easy to explain. He tried somehow, but gave up and repeated the words that he least wanted to say, that there was no harm in it. The Party secretary frowned.

'There is some harm in it,' he replied at last, leafing through the file. 'According to our information, this girl never came to Tirana.'

The playwright laughed.

'Excuse me, but I know this better than anyone.'

The investigator also attempted a smile.

'And we know a bit about our business too.'

'I don't doubt it,' the playwright said. 'But I don't understand what's going on. There's something weird about this story. You summon me to ask about a girl. I admit I have a connection with her. But now you tell me that this connection is impossible because she's never been to Tirana. I'm not contradicting you, but let me ask you, if this is the case, why have you summoned me?'

'To be frank,' the second secretary replied, 'I think there's a misunderstanding here. We may be talking about two different people.'

The investigator searched for something in the file. Rudian and the second secretary watched him, until finally he found what he was looking for.

'I think you will recognise this,' he said, putting a book in front of him.

Rudian slapped himself on the back of the neck.

'I know it very well,' he said. 'And I also remember the dedication with my signature.'

His eyes paused a moment over the inscription: *For Linda B., a souvenir from the author.*

'This is my handwriting and signature. But I've forgotten the name of the girl.'

'So you see now?' the investigator said.

Oh hell, thought the playwright. The letter 'B' had reminded him of something. 'I might say that *you* can see,' he said, not hiding his irritation.

'We've been talking about two different people,' the second secretary repeated.

The playwright felt ready to explode. For no reason at all, he had revealed a secret. Idiot, he thought. He remembered something else, that his unknown reader never came to Tirana. She was someone who read his books but couldn't come to the city, and for this reason wanted a book signed by him.

'I don't understand,' he said. 'You summon me to the Party Committee to ask me if I have a relationship with a girl. Like a fool, I tell you the truth, thinking that the Party is interested in all of this. Then you tell me that this girl can't be the one I love because she's never been to Tirana, and I don't know what to say. Then you show me a book signed by me for another girl, this time one I don't know. I still don't understand what I've done wrong, what the crime is, or what the hell is going on—'

'Slow down,' the second secretary butted in. 'True, there was a misunderstanding on both sides. No harm was intended, but I must tell you that the girl for whom you signed this book and wrote "a souvenir from the author" has, or rather did have, a problem, indeed a serious one.'

The playwright felt a void open up inside him. 'May I ask what kind of problem?'

'Of course you may ask,' came the answer. 'And in fact you should know. The girl is . . . or rather was . . . interned.'

Aha, he thought. He wanted to ask about the strange use of the two tenses, present and past, but a sudden exhaustion suppressed any desire to speak. Of course, he thought . . . being unable to come to Tirana . . . that hindrance . . .

The void inside him expanded. He heard a distant knell toll.

And so? he said to himself, as if in response to that knell.

2

A ND SO? he asked himself again, but quite calmly.
What did this story have to do with him? He'd signed
dozens of books, mostly for strangers. Some murderer
might have had one in his bag, signed before he was led off
in handcuffs, or even after. It was a familiar request: Could
you sign a book for my uncle . . . for my fiancé . . . for a
friend who can't come to Tirana?

He felt a stab under his ribs.

'May I see the book again?' he asked the investigator.

He opened it with his left hand, because his right hand
was shaking. He stared at his own handwriting. The inscription had been written on the first night of his most
recent play, in the foyer immediately afterwards: *For Linda
B., a souvenir from the author. 12th June.*

With blinding clarity he remembered the queue at
the table where he was signing books. An attractive girl
with chestnut hair had caught his eye, and for a reason he
couldn't understand, he speeded up his signing. Perhaps
he was scared that this stranger, for one reason or another,
would change her mind, as beautiful girls usually do, and
leave the queue.

'Could you sign it for a friend who can't be here?'

Without lifting his head, he sensed it was this girl.

Her voice was sweet and as she bent down he thought her long hair was about to touch him . . .

'Her name is Linda. Could you inscribe it for Linda B.?'

'What?' he asked, thinking he had not heard correctly.

'Linda B.,' the girl repeated. 'That's how she would like it.'

As he wrote the dedication, he heard the girl's voice somewhere above him.

'My friend will be thrilled. She adores you.'

He held out the book towards her, and the girl, maintaining her playful gaze, added, 'I'm delighted too.'

And then she had vanished without waiting for his smile.

The playwright returned the book to the investigator.

'I'm certain about the date of the dedication,' he said coldly. 'It was the first night of my play. I don't remember anything else.'

In fact, he did recall their later conversation about the letter 'B':

'What was your friend's fanciful idea with this B?' 'Our imagination had run riot,' the girl had said. 'It had to do with Migjeni's poem addressed to Miss B.'

For the second time, he shook his head to indicate he remembered nothing.

He decided then and there that he would no longer tell the truth, and was surprised how calm this decision made him feel. Nobody deserved it, he thought. Especially not these two at the end of the table. But not just them. Nobody. Starting with his girlfriend. None of them, not even this mysterious girl in internment.

He would behave like they did. This, he thought, would be his salvation. He would become invulnerable and would not communicate with anybody. Let them knock on his door, beg him, curse him, and scream that he had no soul. You do what you want. I'll do what I want. I'll become a sphinx.

Fury took hold of him again, but this time it was different. He thought about Migena. She might have been more honest. She knew her friend was interned and had asked for a book for her. After she had left him, he had gone to his bookshelves to pick up the fallen books and had felt ashamed of what he had done. He was surprised at the depth of his anger. The actual contents of these books, not just their names, seemed to have scattered where they fell, like in an earthquake. Especially one book: *Toponyms*. The names of places, streams, footpaths tumbled on all sides. Cuckoo Hill. The Ambush of the Three Wells. Zeka's Trap, the Pit, the Raven, the Bad Foothills . . . all these grim place names, he thought. There was nothing in this world whose identity, or CV as they now called it, was so repulsive as the land itself. Snares, treachery everywhere . . .

How long had he been in this office of the Party, which he had entered with such unconcern? His eyes wandered to the wall clock that dated back to the friendship with the Chinese. The clock said twenty-seven minutes past ten.

Incredible. He thought he had been there for hours. The Path of the Sprites. The Rough Pass. Wolves. Had they questioned Migena? he wondered. Even if they hadn't, how could these people who knew everything fail to know who this interned girl's friend was?

He felt ashamed of his suspicion, although this did not prevent him from imagining Migena sitting in front of a similar table. What books did this writer have on his shelves? I think you'll remember some of the authors at least. Do you mean the ones that fell when he tried to bash my head against the bookshelves? Not just those. You mean the others too? The books in general. You were there several times and of course you saw them. It's true, I remember some of the names but I didn't know most of the authors. I remember, for instance, Picasso, next to a Heidegger, if I'm not mistaken. The others were new to me.

Speak up. What's the matter?

He thought back to his own questions. Oh God, those questions he'd asked her at their last meeting, like an interrogator.

Something is on your mind. We've talked about it so often. Tell me, what's the matter? I can't bear your tears. Nor those enigmatic phrases of yours: I don't know who you are, my prince or someone else's.

Now it was his turn to ask these questions, he thought. Who do you belong to? Are you my princess or . . . the Party's?

Yet remorse still wormed its way inside him. Perhaps he was being unfair. Perhaps she was suffering too. Perhaps they had interrogated her at night and there was an explanation for all those sighs and tears: she was in two minds, to betray him or not.

A faint cough came like a distant roll of thunder from another age, no doubt a sign for him to break his long silence. They had allowed this silence as a sign of the respect for him that they had mentioned at the start, but he couldn't continue it for ever.

It was possible that it was the other girl, the girl in exile, who had betrayed them. 'You're always going to Tirana, find a book of his, I need one . . .' Or maybe it was neither of them, but a third person.

As if waking up, he raised his head. There was a glint of malice in his interrogators' eyes, like in those place names. The evil eye. In that book of names that fell first after Fitzgerald.

What did it matter to him who was watching him? It wasn't his problem, as people said nowadays. They might find a book signed by him in the bag of some criminal . . . It wasn't the first time that they had harassed him. If they wanted a pretext to condemn his play, let them do what they wanted, just not torture him like this.

As had happened before, he spoke less than half of these words aloud. But they were enough for the second secretary to frown again. This time his frown looked different.

'That is not the problem,' the secretary said quietly. 'It's more complicated than it seems.' He fell silent, then added, 'As I said at the beginning, the Party trusts you just as before. The problem is that the girl we are talking about killed herself.'

Rudian Stefa bit his lower lip, suddenly remembering how they had spoken of her in mixed tenses, sometimes the living present and sometimes the dead past.

'I'm sorry,' he said. 'What a sad story.'

'It's more complicated than that,' said the second secretary. 'I think you know that we take a different view of suicide, especially now.'

In a tired, monotonous voice he explained that since the prime minister's suicide – which, as Rudian well knew, had unravelled the greatest conspiracy in Albanian history – there was a tendency to look for a hidden meaning in every suicide, however apparently straightforward.

'You know', he continued, 'that suicides are intended to give signals and convey messages. Think of Jan Palach in Czechoslovakia, or Stefan Zweig . . . You will know better than I do. We are not ruling out this possibility—'

'Especially because the girl came from a former bourgeois family,' the investigator interrupted. 'Close to the old royal court. Some of the family is in Albania and some abroad. So the investigation will take time.'

The playwright didn't know what to say.

'It's not just a question of the book,' the second secretary said. 'The girl often mentioned your name in her diary.'

'I see,' the playwright replied uncertainly.

'That's the reason why we brought you in,' the secretary said. 'If you think of anything, or remember something that might be useful to the investigation, phone me. Or drop in whenever you like. The Party's door is open.'

'I understand,' the playwright said. 'Of course.'

He was about to stretch out his hand but instead he looked from one man to the other, wondering to whom he should put his last question.

'May I know how long ago this happened?'

The investigator thought for a while.

'Four days ago,' he said. 'Today is day five.'

3

F OUR DAYS ago. Today is day five, he repeated to himself as he walked along the edge of the Park of Youth. He was unable to tell how many days had passed since his last meeting with Migena, on the evening of their quarrel.

Sometimes he counted four, making today day five, but sometimes the result was totally different.

He found himself on the main boulevard opposite the Dajti Hotel. Drinking coffee there among foreigners seemed even more unwise than ever. Don't pretend life's still the same, he told himself. It was Llukan Herri who had invented what their circle of close friends called 'the Dajti test'. When you're not sure you feel totally safe in your own skin, pass in front of the Dajti Hotel. If your feet hesitate even for an instant before entering, forget it. Admit that you're no longer safe, to put it mildly.

The National Gallery next door to the hotel was closed. The Writers' Club on the other side of the street offered a test of a different kind. By a strange coincidence, everybody who was marked for prison visited the bar more frequently before fate struck.

It was eleven o'clock and he was standing by the entrance to the theatre. The old posters had been torn down and not replaced. Tirana had never looked so forlorn.

It seemed incredible to him that three months ago he had signed that book in the midst of the cheerful first-night hubbub.

Migena had phoned him a week later. 'Hello. I'm an art student. I'm sorry to bother you, but it was me who asked you for an autograph for her friend. Perhaps you remember?'

He had said that he remembered her very well, and the tone of the girl's low voice at the end of the phone brightened. Her friend had been delighted with the book. He couldn't imagine how happy it had made her. She herself too, of course.

They met two days later, and again her first words were about her friend, but when he said that next time the two girls might come together if they liked, her eyes momentarily froze. Of course her friend would be thrilled, really thrilled, but right now . . . she couldn't. 'I understand,' he had said, although he hadn't understood anything at all. Was something stopping this girl coming to the capital?

He felt someone's presence behind him and a stranger's voice asked, 'No performances this week?' 'See for yourself,' he replied, without turning his head.

Despite his resistance, his feet then turned him back towards the Writers' Club. Let happen what may, he thought.

At first he assumed the main room of the club was empty, but as he sat down he noticed the familiar face of a writer in the far corner. He wanted to say hello, but the writer did not see him, or pretended not to. If you don't want to speak, don't bother, he thought, and sat down, turning his back to the writer. People had a point when they said of this man that he directed most of his anger at the wrong targets. Especially since he had published that ill-fated book, *The Winter of Bitter Winds*.

Rudian tried not to think about him. He would have liked merely to tell the man that he had no reason to look so gloomy, especially in his presence. Two or three times, Rudian had almost got into trouble for things this writer had said, such as the business about cells in the front of the brain being damaged or dead.

It was enough to drive you crazy. Llukan Herri had asked him one day: 'Was it you talking about the cells in the front of the brain, the ones that should invent new things in art?' When Rudian shook his head, Llukan had gone on to say that it must have been that other writer, who goes on about rain and the wind, with whom they'd been confusing him recently.

He groaned to himself, finally turning his mind back to the girl.

Migena's icy expression became even more inexplicable on reflection, as happened to most things in the Writers' Club. How could he have taken her look so lightly? All his concentration and haste had been focused less on what she said than on the beautiful shape of her lips and his impatience to kiss them. But that coldness had reappeared after his kisses, and even after her kisses, which were the sweetest of all. He had wanted to ask her what was troubling her, but gently, without creating alarm, as one might ask a naive lover worried about a broken promise.

Looking back, he was astonished not at her but at his own naivety. Particularly when, a few days after, the iciness in her eyes could be felt in her breath and seen in her shoulders. In the moments before she undressed, it had been so obvious that he had wondered if she might be a virgin.

The girl had answered vaguely, neither yes nor no, with conditional verbs: even if I were, it wouldn't be a problem. But her transfixed expression remained the same. After making love, instead of calming down, she grew worse. She lay for a while with her face deep in the pillow and he would have thought she was asleep but for her shoulders, which trembled with increasingly strong emotion. He tried to draw her to him, at least to see her face, but the girl gripped the pillow with her naked arms.

He asked her again what was worrying her, but less cautiously than before. It wasn't about being a virgin, that was now clear. So what was it? Had she promised to be faithful to some boy, or was it some other nonsense? Well?

A faint rustle of her hair indicated no, and she said haltingly that it wasn't a question of fidelity or any other nonsense, but something else.

I see, so she's starting to play games, he thought.

'What is it then?' he asked coldly.

Her reply was unexpected. It was better if he didn't know.

'I see,' Rudian said, this time aloud.

Immediately his thoughts turned to the anxiety of the last few days over the new postponement of his play. He wanted to say to her: Do you remember that premiere where we met, with all the excitement in the foyer? And now this is the second time a play of mine has been postponed at the last moment. And you go on complaining about who knows what silliness.

Propped up on his elbow, he studied her bare shoulders with a certain indifferent ease that he believed came from being known to the public. He hadn't felt suspicious, especially because their conversation about that other unknown girl had been in passing, in a bantering tone, and with no sense of drama.

'When are you going to introduce me to that friend of yours?' 'I don't know. Do you really want to meet her?' 'Why not? You haven't mentioned her in a while.' 'Perhaps because I don't know what to tell you. I really don't, except that . . .' 'Except what?' 'Except that . . . she's prettier than me.' 'Aha . . .'

The coffee tasted bitter. Migena's anxiety did not diminish, and became even more mysterious.

'Is this coffee different from usual?' he asked the waiter.

The waiter shrugged his shoulders.

He had said to her quite coolly that if their meetings were going to end in floods of tears it would be better not to see each other anymore. Her eyes sank even deeper into misery. Just don't ever say that again, she had whispered. Never, do you hear me? Never.

'It's the same coffee,' the waiter said, taking the cup. 'Vietnamese.'

Rudian was sure that Migena's unhappiness was about something unrelated to him, which he would never discover, just as he would never see this other wretched girl.

'Shall I bring you another coffee?' the waiter asked. 'Not heated for so long. It'll taste different.'

'No, thank you,' Rudian replied. 'I have to go.'

As he stood up, the writer watched Rudian from his seat in the corner, as if about to greet him. Rudian pretended to take no notice.

Still there was no poster by the theatre entrance. Better not to know. This phrase presented itself in his mind, unconnected to anything specific. Not to know what? The things they would say or had already said at the Artistic Board, and which he hadn't yet heard? Of course, he thought, but then he recalled that it was someone else who had first uttered these words to him.

What was he better off not knowing about? he wondered. He was now angrier at himself than at the girl. He had heard these words and accepted them meekly. He should have responded in totally the opposite way. The bed where they made love was a more suitable place for a confession than any other.

What the hell was it that he shouldn't know? That they were asking her about him at the Investigator's Office? About the next play he intended to write? About his battles with his conscience over betraying her? All that?

Above his head, the city-centre clock struck noon. However hard you try to elude me, I will track you down, he said to himself.

Wherever you hide, he added.

Fleeing the tones of the bell, he turned back towards the entrance to the Dajti Hotel, where he hesitated only briefly. He climbed the steps and passed disdainfully through the silent lobby, watched by the receptionists. Beyond the door to the bar, the counter loomed up in front of him.

He sat down and noticed that the bar was half empty.

You and your enigmas, he thought drowsily. And suddenly, waking up, he made a discovery. The name 'Migena' and the word 'enigma' fluttered through his mind, attempting to come together. They were anagrams. Migena, enigma. To make sure, he wrote the words on the menu, next to the words 'espresso coffee'. Yes, they really were anagrams. Yes: shuffle the letters of 'Migena' and you got 'enigma'.

4

SEVEN DAYS. This is day eight, he thought, sipping coffee a few days later at the same table in the Dajti. To his right, the director of the theatre, who was sitting with the members of the Cuban cultural delegation recently arrived in Tirana, craned his neck as if to make sure that the man quietly drinking coffee three tables away really was Rudian Stefa, the playwright with one premiere temporarily postponed and another play waiting approval.

If you want to turn half of the state institutions in Albania upside down, his friend Llukan Herri used to say, drink your coffee in the Dajti at the very time you don't feel safe. According to Llukan, each state agency would think that another one knew why the dramatist R.S. had drunk coffee in the Dajti for several days in a row without batting an eyelid. For instance, the director of the theatre, instead of concentrating on the recent instructions delivered by Fidel Castro in a six-hour speech to the actors of Havana, would rack his brains for an explanation for Rudian Stefa's boldness, and might suspect that the criticisms of Stefa's most recent play that the director intended to put before the Artistic Board were too harsh.

Rudian stifled a sigh of such force that it seemed to kick against his ribs, unleashing an unpleasant wave of dizziness.

Why should I care about all this? he thought. Let them think what they want, I have no business with them. Nor did he need the mean-spirited pleasure that he had enjoyed five minutes ago, speculating about the qualms of the theatre director as he listened to the pearls from Castro's speech. Let them do what they want, so long as they don't touch my play . . . and . . . also . . . don't keep Migena from me.

The realisation that they could keep Migena from him flashed through his mind. But it was followed immediately by the thought that nobody was keeping her away. She had left him of her own accord.

A great weariness, like some mist from far away, seemed to have settled between them. It was a long time since he had fallen in love, although he wondered if this were not love but something else that had donned love's familiar mask to deceive him.

She was avoiding him and soon she would become almost a stranger to him, the perfect stranger who would never be forgotten. He strove to recall her palpable form but already this was not easy. He could not even remember her body below the waist. Had she ever let him see it? At first he had interpreted this as her provincial shyness, but later he suspected something else.

He fumbled nervously in his jacket's right-hand pocket for the letter that she had placed on the pillow before she left their last meeting but one. 'There's a letter for you on the bed,' she had whispered in his ear, before fleeing downstairs as if scared he might follow her. *Who are you? Are you really my prince?* These words had been scrawled in red ballpoint in the semi-darkness after their lovemaking. The question *Who are you?* was repeated at the end, with another question: *And me, who am I?*

He longed not only to fold her in his arms, in the usual way of men throughout the world, whether in socialist republics, confederations, kingdoms or prince-bishoprics. He wanted to howl again and again as he had done by his bookshelves, among the streams, crags and chasms with those treacherous names.

'Revolutionary Cuban theatre, under the teaching of Fidel Castro, is advancing towards new developments . . .' What was that? He turned his head towards the now empty table where the Cuban cultural delegation had been sitting, astonished to hear their conversation again. Before he suspected himself of losing his wits, he saw the barman fiddle with the radio and turn down the volume.

He motioned to the passing waiter and asked if this was still the radio programme about Cuban theatre. The waiter nodded. It was the same one. Day four.

His mind returned to the girl.

If she could ask him who he was, how had it not occurred to him to find out more about her? He had started on enigmas and anagrams but it struck him that he didn't even know her surname. He had learned nothing from her but a little about her first sexual experience.

'It was our gym teacher, as so often in schools. Two or three of us girls had been together since the third form. We thought we couldn't say no because he was the only man who had seen us in our underwear . . . Only one of us, your Linda.' 'Who?' 'I told you once, that's what her friends called her . . . So my girlfriend stood up to him. Not that she was a prude, not at all, but because she was different, in every way . . .'

Idiot, he snorted to himself. What an idiot to listen to this sort of thing without caring. He reproached himself again but with less conviction, realising that without the summons to the Party Committee and all that followed he would have known nothing about this girl.

He ordered another coffee and thought that the waiter was looking at him with increased respect. New customers had entered the bar. He tried to forget everything, at least for the duration of his second coffee. But this made matters worse. As he tried to forget the Artistic Board of the theatre, his mind still turned back to the girl.

If I could just see her once more . . .

What a cheap, superficial, semi-articulate idea without depth or mystery, not worthy of respect. He knew this and yet he repeated it: If I could just see her once more. Only once. He wasn't sure if he would wail at her – Who are you? – or lovingly embrace her as he had in a time that now seemed so distant.

Abruptly he stood up and went to the counter.

'May I use the phone?'

'Of course,' the barman replied with unconcealed surprise.

Rudian Stefa was surprised at himself. All Tirana knew that the phones in the Dajti were tapped, but this didn't deter him. He dialled the investigator's number carefully, pausing to ask himself what he was doing only when he had nearly finished. But this question, far from restraining him, had the opposite effect. 'Hello, this is Rudian Stefa.'

The voice down the wire sounded friendly. Distracted, Rudian imagined rather than listened to the investigator's polite words, and tried to make it clear that he was not phoning to report anything. Perhaps this might be a disappointment, but he was phoning for no reason at all, just to extend an invitation for coffee.

The investigator understood even before Rudian had said half of this and was quicker off the mark with his own invitation. Would he have time for a coffee?

'I'd be delighted,' Rudian replied. In some confusion he heard the man mention a place he didn't call the cake shop, but 'Café Flora', as it had once been known before the ideological campaign against cafés.

Rudian was struck less by the investigator's friendly manner than by his total lack of professional inquisitiveness. He hadn't expressed the slightest disappointment at Rudian's 'for no reason'. In fact he had almost welcomed it with relief.

What am I letting myself in for? he asked himself as he passed the marble colonnade of the Palace of Culture, his mind dogged by the thought that he was going like a lamb to the slaughter. Passing the National Museum, he had even wondered aloud, 'What are you doing?' Was he attracted to a game that he liked to think was dangerous, but wasn't really? He knew that none of this was for no reason, as he had tried to deceive himself a short time ago at the crossroads of Dibra Street from where Skanderbeg's bronze horse loomed so grim in the distance. His mind was hazy, but he was aware what lay behind this mist: Migena. From afar, the red sign of Café Flora glinted perilously. Nobody in the world would find out what he might do to this girl. Protect her, or the contrary: hand her in. Even if he wanted to do one of these things, neither was possible. No doubt they knew everything about her. He was totally uninvolved in the case. That was why he was in no hurry and the investigator was so courteously indifferent.

The windows of the café drew closer, and soon he would see his own wavering reflection in them. Perhaps everything was simpler than it seemed. He dimly remembered a story by Chekhov or Gogol in which a man stroked the neck of a horse and talked to it because he could not find a single human being with whom he could share his sorrow.

It is like that, he thought as he pushed open the glass door. In this desert, he had found the only person who knew something about his infinite grief, and who might tell him something, or could perhaps help him find the girl again . . .

Surely that was it, nothing else. He wanted her back with him, to rest his head on her lovely breasts and then on her stomach, and on the edge of that dark abyss where he might still find out things about her he was yet to discover.

5

THE INVESTIGATOR sat waiting in the far right corner of the café, at what had been Rudian's favourite table for years. Rudian stretched out his hand and was about to remark on the coincidence, but it occurred to him that it might be nothing of the sort. The investigator would know as well as he did where he liked to sit. As all Tirana knew, the Flora came second after the Dajti for microphones under the tables.

The investigator's smile provided a natural backdrop to their polite exchanges: how nice to see you, it's my pleasure, perhaps I'm taking up your time, on the contrary, how delightful, particularly now that . . . Cuban theatre, under the teachings of Fidel Castro, has been very successful, especially when . . . why is that radio so loud . . . we need to take a break from routine sometimes . . . *revoluthion*, only *revoluthion* . . . excuse me, could you turn down that radio . . . 'Would you like a coffee?'

Instead of saying he had just drunk two, Rudian asked a question that he knew immediately was a mistake: 'Are you busy these days?'

'You might say so,' the investigator replied quite naturally, discounting any possibility of having misinterpreted the question. 'We've plenty to do,' meaning waves of arrests, conspiracies. Watch out . . .

Perhaps now the investigator would retaliate with his own irritating enquiry: How's the writing going? Followed by that other fatal question: What are you working on at the moment?

Rudian imagined his reply, that the Artistic Board was considering a play of his. He could add without flattery: I would rather it were in your hands than theirs. At least the investigators would give it their expert attention, looking for hostile catchphrases, counting the number of lines given to negative characters as against positive ones, looking at the fingerprints on the manuscript to find out if anyone suspicious had read it. All this would be preferable to the assessment by the Artistic Board, where for the third time the sticking point was an appearance of the partisan's ghost at the end of Act Two. Rudian had heard that the majority of the Board had not only insisted that socialist realism didn't allow ghosts, but that the matter went deeper and had to do with some dangerous influences recently evident. Ugh . . .

'There are problems in the theatre, like everywhere,' Rudian said. 'We heard just now on the radio about revolutionary theatre in Cuba.'

'Really? I wasn't listening,' the investigator responded. 'I was merely thinking of how the radio was bothering us.'

'I know. Our theatre has invited a Cuban delegation on an official visit. These Cuban comrades told us that Fidel Castro spoke for six hours about issues in the Havana theatre.'

'Really?' the investigator said.

'Can you imagine, six hours? Setting aside all the affairs of state. This business must be so complicated that . . .'

The investigator looked at him blankly. 'I go to the theatre and read as much as I can, but to tell the truth I'm not very clued up,' he said slowly.

'I understand.'

'You are one of the few people from the arts whom I've had a chance to meet. On this occasion, unfortunately, for other reasons.'

'I understand,' Rudian said again, while thinking: Now, at last. The investigator was getting close to what Rudian had been waiting for with such impatience.

Neither spoke a word for a long time. They sipped their coffees and Rudian was ready for a fourth, or even a fifth, until his temples thudded from caffeine, if only this man would speak.

The investigator's silence cut into Rudian's very soul. They must learn these tricks at those academies of theirs, just as students at Migena's art college picked up the techniques of the stage: long pauses, yawns that simulate indifference, coughs.

'Some new play?' he said at last, in that special bright tone reserved for hope for the future, and often used with visibly pregnant women you met in the street . . . Expecting a little one, are we?

'Not yet,' Rudian replied doubtfully. 'In fact I have a play ready, but it's still with the Artistic Board.' It was hard to resist asking: Do you know why? You have forensic expertise, you deal in facts. You might not credit that it's stuck there because of a ghost.

'As I said, I'm fond of the theatre, especially – as you may imagine – when plays deal with subjects close to our work: investigations, conundrums . . .'

Rudian barely contained a sigh. This was all he needed, after a six-hour speech by Fidel Castro: more wittering about the theatre. Apparently the investigator was not feigning ignorance, but this realisation, instead of reassuring him, merely drove him to despair. If the investigator had been pretending, he could be expected to open up, but now there was no hope he would talk frankly.

Well, if the investigator was not going to start, Rudian himself would have to speak up first. He couldn't care less if it was interpreted as impatience, or worse.

He looked the man straight in the eye and said, 'Thinking of what we talked about at the Party Committee . . . I haven't found out anything new. Perhaps I've disappointed you—'

'Not at all,' the investigator butted in. 'You made that quite clear on the phone. You said we would meet for no reason at all.' There was amusement in his expression. 'I wanted to say what a pleasure it is for me to have coffee with you. An unusual opportunity. My colleagues will be jealous.'

Rudian kicked himself. You idiot. You got yourself into this mess. Let's meet for coffee, for no reason. Then you complain when this man doesn't open up.

Now his temples were beating. He'd never drunk such strong coffee. Instead of listening to the investigator, his mind wandered to Caligula and the horse that he made consul. The emperor would whisper state secrets into the horse's ear, about the affairs of Rome and conspiracies soon to be exposed, telling the animal which senators would be given orders to cut their veins on Tuesday night, and which on Wednesday, like that irritating dramatist Seneca. Let them be a lesson to everybody . . .

'While we're on the subject, how did that business go?' Rudian asked, keeping his gaze steady.

The investigator calmly returned his stare, but with a look of surprise, and asked what business he had in mind.

'What we talked about at the Party Committee. The girl who killed herself.'

'Ah, I see,' the investigator said.

'She came from an old bourgeois family close to the former royal court, if I'm not mistaken. You said that suicides of this sort are always treated with suspicion.'

'Of course,' the investigator said. 'You're quite right.'

Quite right, Rudian repeated to himself. Then why the hell doesn't he say something?

'Investigations are still ongoing?'

'Of course.'

Investigations . . . of course. But nothing about Migena, her close friend, who went to and from Tirana for her, carrying books and messages, perhaps in code.

Rudian looked sidelong at the investigator's face. Clearly he didn't like this turn in the conversation. Incredibly, their roles were now reversed. Any other investigator, pursuing a clue about a conspiracy or rebellion, about an Albanian Jan Palach, would have risen in the middle of the night from his bed, whether marital or solitary, to answer a witness's phone call, and would have run through snow and rain, brimming over with gratitude, to fall to his knees in front of his informant. But this one was as silent as a mummy.

His answers came slowly. He had no desire to pry. What a strange kind of investigator – nervous, even terrified of discovering anything.

Rudian Stefa thrust his hands in his pockets to stop himself fidgeting. As always, this made him feel confident.

'Please don't get me wrong,' he said in an icy voice. 'I'm asking about this because it's connected to one of my books, if you follow me. You summoned me to the Party Committee about this problem. I have a right to know. I'm not sure if you understand me.'

'I see what you mean,' the investigator replied.

'And so?'

Rudian wanted to ask why the other man had kept so silent and caused him such anxiety.

The investigator studied him thoughtfully, unprepared for this sudden turn in the conversation. Rudian waited for an explanation before giving in to annoyance.

He tried to think back to Caligula's horse, or more precisely to the emperor himself, snorting as he remembered Seneca. He had tolerated that wayward playwright for long enough, with his irritating Greek influences. And now this writer was putting ghosts on the stage again. This was all Rome needed. It would be the ruin of the city. Caligula was not the sort to make six-hour speeches about the problems of the theatre. He would settle matters quickly. A centurion would knock that very night on the writer's door. Seneca would not live to see the dawn.

'You're right to be worried,' the investigator said quietly. 'This case is still under investigation.'

Dead before dawn, thought Rudian. What was that in Latin?

Rudian watched the investigator attentively. Had his expression relaxed a little? Twice in the last year Rudian had been forced to stand up and make self-criticism for his hot temper, and he had no desire to do it again.

'As for the suicide, we looked at the files and it turns out it had nothing to do with politics. The reasons were private and personal.'

So the reasons were personal, thought Rudian. But strong enough to break the mainspring of her life.

'I see,' he said.

'As for your book, it's true that it was a striking piece of evidence. I don't know if I told you that the girl also made notes about you in her diary.'

'Really?'

'Admiring comments and rather more than that. One might say she had tender feelings towards you.'

'I see.'

'So there's your answer.' The investigator spread his arms and gave Rudian a curious look.

'Strange . . .' Rudian said in an uncertain voice.

'What do you mean, strange?' the investigator asked. 'You know better than I do that girls often have these feelings.'

'It's true, they often do. But a girl who is interned, from a family of this kind. I don't think this happens often.'

They fell silent, and both toyed nervously with their coffee cups.

The appearance at the end of Act Two of the ghost of the partisan shot in the back by the edge of the marsh came again to his mind. For the last few days, Rudian had been brooding about him, considering him from different angles – favourable or not – trying to work out what impression he would create on the members of the Board as they read the script.

'We still don't know each other well,' Rudian said. 'But may I ask you a question that is, how shall I put it, direct – that is . . . awkward?' The investigator's eyes froze as he listened. 'Am I under surveillance?'

The investigator shivered.

'No,' he said curtly. 'On my word of honour, although perhaps you won't believe that someone in my profession has such a thing. On my word of honour, you're not being watched in any way.'

The investigator's look was indecipherable, strangely downcast, and not at all triumphant. 'I will try to explain,' he said slowly. 'I think you will understand me.'

6

A N HOUR later they were both still there. Each of them glanced repeatedly at his watch but neither wanted to go. As if honouring a pact, they had reverted to small talk, but the words the investigator had said a short time ago still ran through Rudian's mind. This short discussion had confirmed certain things that he had long suspected. The investigators knew what he thought about Stalin, about the theatre and the ban on religion. They knew his acid jokes at the expense of Politburo members. He had no reason to be surprised at this or to think that the Party was going soft. His situation was unchanged, because, although it was never made explicit, there were two different yardsticks for the measurement of offences. An army officer or loyal communist would be sentenced to prison, if not shot, for the least criticism of Stalin, the ban on religion, or the Politburo. But for people like him, such opinions were not considered dangerous. A specific office analysed these matters over the years, like a laboratory comparing blood samples or X-rays. The office would ask: What do people think of Stalin? And the data would come in, showing the same reservations as two years ago.

Religion: stable. Politburo: deteriorating. We've added the name of B.B. to our list. We thought he was above board because he's an engineer, but he's turned out to be just like the other idiots. In education, primary schools are doing rather better. There has been no criticism of the big chief.

This was the most important and decisive indicator, the test of malignancy.

Even in the offices of the Security Service the employees found it hard to understand. They muttered about it day and night. Why were some so cossetted, while others got it in the neck? The staff thought they had every right to feel aggrieved. They had worn themselves out gathering this incriminating poison, and nobody paid any attention to it. The poison turned out to be harmless! But why in some cases and not in others?

To keep them quiet, it had been necessary to threaten and imprison them. Shut up. The Party knows best. And they did keep quiet. They could do nothing else. But this didn't prevent them gnashing their teeth: the rat's got away one more time.

'I'm sorry, this was the exact phrase they used about you.'

'Of course,' Rudian replied. But he wondered why the investigator was telling him this in such detail. Was this honesty, or a threat? Possibly both. But so what? he thought. Nothing more was going to happen.

He's got away from us . . . the rat . . . So that's how they talked about him. He had been aware of this, more or less, but it was different hearing it at first hand.

Amazingly, he did not crumple. He only felt stronger. Like someone who, already soaked, thinks nothing of a downpour. They had been watching him for a long time and still not touched him.

And yet he could not feel totally calm. There was part of him that could not be reassured. Why, really, had he asked for this meeting? He tried to recall the moment when he had stood up to ask for the phone in the bar of the Dajti Hotel. He couldn't remember what he had been thinking of as he went over to the counter. There had been nothing in his mind, only a mist behind which lay, as if veiled, the dim shape of a woman.

Why had he sought this meeting? The question came back to him, this time with a pang of guilt.

Speak, like Caligula. Tell the horse about her breasts and what lay between her thighs, that space you never fully enjoyed.

The investigator, as if knowing from long experience that he was going to say something, remained totally silent.

'Do you remember that day when you summoned me to the Party Committee? Strange, how long ago it seems. You remember, I talked to you about a girl . . . In fact, I was so sure that you had asked me to come because of her that I jumped to conclusions and talked about her far too quickly.'

The investigator screwed up his eyes as if to assist his memory.

'Yes,' he said, 'I remember.'

Rudian waited for him to continue, and imagined him producing phrases along the lines of, To tell the truth, I was a little surprised too. Or, Yes, why did you mention that girl? How easy it would have been to keep the conversation going. Any playwright could do it. But the investigator showed no curiosity.

He wanted to shriek: What the hell is the matter? What sort of investigator are you? Does this mean nothing to you? Ask me about her!

A familiar wave of fury that he knew he was powerless to stem swept over him.

Filthy trade, he railed to himself. When you want to, you probe any sort of nonsense – what old Xija says in the milk queue, which widow the lame doorman at the theatre is screwing – but when a really fine story comes along you close your ears. Go on, he appealed again. Are you made of stone, are you a horse? Why not say something?

For the first time, he weakened. He was reduced to this, he thought. He was worse off than the Russian cart-driver in the steppes. At least Chekhov's peasant of the plains had confessed to his horse. His luck was to open his heart to an Albanian investigator.

'I see you're upset,' the investigator said. 'I don't understand why.'

'It's nothing,' Rudian replied. 'Nothing at all. It's my fault.'

'Honestly, I don't understand you.'

'I don't understand you either.'

Rudian could hardly contain the urge to tell him to his face, You pretend to be frank with me but you're nothing of the sort, and then to ask the simple, specific question: Why not ask me about her? I gave you the cue myself, and you pretend not to understand. Why not? Say something. Only if she . . .

An old suspicion came back to him. In after-dinner conversations, it was often said that in any group of four people one was a spy. Some believed it and others considered it an invention of the Security Service itself, intended to spread fear. Now it seemed more probable than ever. They didn't want to hear about the girl because she was one of their own.

His anger was plain to see, but he couldn't care less. The radio played popular songs from the south: *Grow, my little almond tree, in the cypress shade.* He thought it was that one, but couldn't be sure. A song with a similar tune, heard one afternoon on the train between Rrogozhina and Lushnja, suddenly came to his mind:

> *Girl from Kolonja*
> *In Roskovec born and bred*
> *Why did you drink Chinese poison?*
> *For now you are dead.*

His nerves were frayed. Finally, he told the investigator if not the gist, at least a part of what he had wanted to say, and in a very obscure fashion. He had, by accident,

45

told him an intimate secret and the man had shown no interest. Of course, he was not obliged to do so, but still, it was strange behaviour from anyone, and especially from an investigator.

The investigator listened with concern.

'I'm sorry if you took it in this way,' he said. 'But believe me, it was not intended.' The investigator was also no longer clear. 'I meant it quite differently . . . in fact in the opposite way . . . as you might say, out of respect for you . . . especially as your secret came out, as you said yourself, by accident.'

Rudian stared as he listened. The investigator was entirely right, but pride would not let him apologise. The clumsy thought passed through his mind that her breasts were just as sweet whether she was an informer or not. And her tears too. Especially her tears. Besides, how could a police informer weep so movingly? It was of course impossible. But then the opposite thought, that this was precisely the reason why she had wept, disoriented him again.

This was his final suspicion.

A melting sensation spread through his chest, perhaps from the exhaustion of this endless day.

'I've never seen her since,' he said softly.

What am I doing? he thought. He then put the question to himself again, as if it were being asked by someone else from the wings of a stage. What do you think you're doing?

The investigator listened, not taking his eyes off Rudian, still quiet as before and with no sign of professional inquisitiveness.

'She was beautiful,' Rudian said. 'I mean, she is . . . I hope she hasn't changed.'

What am I doing? he said to himself again. But still he kept talking. 'There was something enigmatic about that girl, something elusive, that you couldn't grasp . . . Still, I was sure that she'd really fallen in love with me.'

With a sort of fastidiousness, perhaps prompted by the long silence, the investigator intervened:

'You artists and writers are lucky with women. In fact, I sometimes think that these occasional outbursts of resentment against writers come from envy, or more exactly, envy of your success with women.'

'I also think that I loved her,' Rudian said, seeming not to hear what the other man had said. 'For a long time I thought I'd lost the ability to fall in love.'

He screwed up his eyes as if suddenly remembering something, stared at the tabletop and muttered to himself. 'I thought about that for a long time.' Then he turned to the investigator with a changed expression. 'My impression is that you are aware of this.'

The investigator leaned forward as if to hear better.

'What should I be aware of?'

'They were both from the same small town. I mean, my friend Migena and that girl. My friend probably took my book to her . . . I'm sure you realise that.'

His voice was almost hoarse.

The investigator sat motionless.

'Let's suppose that was the case,' he said at last. 'Then what?'

'Then what? What do you mean, then what?' Rudian burst out. 'You pretended to be honest with me. If that was the case, if you really were being upfront, you should have asked me questions. Looked for explanations.'

'I don't understand.'

'I understand even less. If you knew that my friend had taken the book to where the girl was interned . . . why didn't you say something to me?'

'Let's suppose we did know,' the investigator replied. 'Why should we question you? I mean, why should we cause you anxiety?'

'Thank you so much! Why should we cause you anxiety, you say. What a gentleman!'

'No need for sarcasm. I explained to you a while back how things are, where personalities like you are concerned. I told you in all honesty that it's not up to us to decide.'

'If that's so, why did you summon me?'

'As you know, you weren't summoned to the Investigator's Office, but to the Party Committee. Second, the most important thing about this case is that it was initially taken very seriously. I told you a little about it. There was a suspicion of something really big, with royalist émigrés involved, even the king himself.'

'And then? What happened after that? Was that dismissed?'

'More or less.'

'I see . . . Anyway, we don't understand each other,' Rudian said. 'We belong to different worlds. Let me ask you a question. I promise you, it's the last. Then I'll leave you alone. The question is about Migena, the girl we talked about. Is she, or was she, your informer?'

For the first time the investigator did not hide his annoyance.

'No,' he said curtly. He picked up his cup and raised it to his lips, even though it was empty. Then he lowered it in angry haste. 'No.' He shook his head, avoiding Rudian's look. The investigator himself seemed to have the greater need for this denial.

Rudian also looked away.

'Who knows what you did to the poor thing,' he said quietly. 'You must have scared her. You must have made her sick.'

The investigator shook his head.

'Not at all.'

Rudian could barely restrain his bitter smile.

'I can understand your surprise,' the investigator said. 'But I'll try to explain, because I respect you. And this is for the last time.'

So much the better, thought Rudian, to end this torture as soon as possible.

7

THE INVESTIGATOR'S speech slid into an indistinct drawl. Of course investigators were no angels, he said. This wasn't Monte Carlo, but the dictatorship of the proletariat. Yet sometimes, as in cases like his, or in similar ones like that of this student – his girlfriend – they showed extreme care. I see, Rudian said to himself. So their respect for him ran even deeper. The investigator asked Rudian to understand him correctly. It was not solely for his sake. The fact that she was his lover played a part, but that wasn't enough in itself. There was another reason. Rudian was curious about this other reason but could not help noticing the words the investigator used for the girl – not her name but his 'lover', 'the girl you love' or, more rarely, his 'girlfriend'. (Who are you? Are you my prince or someone else's?) She had never used these words except perhaps in one of her two letters (And me, who am I? Am I really your lover . . . as you might say . . . your princess?).

They had handled this girl with caution, the investigator said, because of someone other than himself. Rudian tried to concentrate. It was because of Migena's father. He was an unsung hero, someone who had silently put himself in the service of the revolution and asked for nothing in return. Rudian started paying more attention. Migena's father was still young, in his forties. He had been pensioned early, and he was injured not so much by the bullets in his body as by mental damage. An assassin, Rudian thought. One of the state's hitmen. They usually ended up like that, marginalised but treated with special honour. Of course his daughter would not be closely investigated. This also explained her friendship with the other girl, who was an internee. She lived in a small town, so hers was not a classic kind of internment – not like being exiled to the villages of Lushnja, or being sent to a camp. But it was still internment: reporting to the police every evening and all the rest. Even though she went to high school, nobody else would dare make friends with her as Migena had done. They were top of the class at school, and also, no doubt, the prettiest.

The ghost of the partisan on the edge of the marsh at the end of Act Two appeared, motionless, in Rudian's mind.

Her father and her lover, both handled with kid gloves, he thought.

He couldn't muster another bitter smile. His possible father-in-law, privileged for his extreme loyalty, and he himself, the possible son-in-law, privileged for his possible disloyalty. Rock solid. He'd heard that expression for the first time at a birthday party some years before. In our family we have four Party members, two war dead, and an ambassador. Rock solid, aren't we? In contrast to a certain other person, they muttered under their breath. Amazingly beautiful girl, but what can you do, a dodgy family. Father shot, and a priest at that. Two aunts interned. Uncle in prison.

'Shall we have another?' the investigator said. 'I could drink one more coffee.'

Of course, Rudian thought. Till two in the morning, perhaps three. Maybe you'll interrogate a bishop next. If there are any left.

Again he felt drained, exhausted.

'And her suicide?' he said softly. 'What happened?'

The investigator's expression became sombre.

He's clammed up, Rudian thought. There's no more.

The investigator hesitated, and for the first time did not conceal it.

'That's a different question,' he said at last.

Rudian waited for more, until he realised that was all the other man would say.

'Was it a private matter?'

The investigator waved a flattened hand to indicate 'sort of'.

'Anyway . . .' Rudian said. 'I wanted to know.'

The investigator looked him in the eyes.

'Better if you don't know,' he said.

Rudian felt a stab in his heart. This was the second time he'd heard this phrase. He was too angry to think clearly. What business of his own was this story? Why was he suddenly being treated as a part of it, as if for one reason or another he had something to hide? What does this mean? he shouted to himself. Did he alone have no right to ask what was going on? Why this fatherly care, shielding him from anxiety? They could keep these scruples to themselves, or for that crippled hero of theirs, who wasn't yet his father-in-law.

The waiter, to whom the investigator had apparently gestured, stood expecting a new order.

'Don't you have any other coffee besides this Vietnamese stuff?' Rudian asked with annoyance. 'Anything else, just not Vietnamese.'

The waiter shrugged his shoulders.

'Go and ask the manager,' the investigator said gently.

Rudian tried to catch the investigator's eye again. Had he really glimpsed an expression of sympathy a few moments ago, or had it been an illusion? He didn't need anybody's sympathy, least of all this man's. What responsibility did he have if a girl he'd never seen had killed herself five hundred miles away? Let the man keep his sympathy for somebody else, if he even knows what that feeling is. Does he think he can make me feel guilty for giving this girl an inscribed book? Who knows what this idiot investigator and all these other fools are thinking. Do they imagine that writers are such sissies that, if they hurt a sparrow, they suffer pangs of conscience for months? Cretin. Didn't he know how cruel writers can be? If their roles were reversed, Rudian Stefa wouldn't interrogate with this delicacy. He would shackle the man's hands behind his chair back and scream at this filthy state torturer: Tell us how you gouged out Father Meshkalla's eyes because he baptised a baby; tell us how you ripped up a painter's canvases with scissors before his very eyes, while he shouted, 'Cut off my fingers, but leave my pictures alone,' and so on, for forty years on end.

'There's only the Vietnamese,' the waiter said, sounding guilty.

'Whatever it is, bring one coffee,' the investigator said. 'Perhaps you'd prefer hot chocolate,' he said to Rudian. 'It's not bad here.'

Rudian nodded. To hell with this, he thought. The only thing waiters ever did properly was interrupt his train of thought. He was looking at the investigator's hands and thinking about handcuffs. That's how he would question him, handcuffed, while force-feeding him torrents of Vietnamese coffee and making him listen to six-hour radio speeches by Fidel Castro. You were so sensitive, so delicate, so careful not to cause offence when mentioning the inscription in that book. Well, don't expect the same from us writers.

From us, he repeated to himself. Why get so agitated? We have nothing. They have the handcuffs. We just dream of them.

The investigator's eyes now seemed fixed on his own hands. No doubt, like every investigator, he had handcuffs in his pocket. Rudian knew from reading about Russian dissidents that arrests happened in the most incredible places. In the cinema, for example: the man sitting next to you laughing in the most simple-minded way at the film, and you think that at least there are some happy people in this world who can enjoy anything. This man suddenly slides the handcuffs from his pocket and there is the steel round your right wrist.

It would be quite normal for this to happen right there at the table with the cups of Vietnamese coffee at the Café Flora, Durrës Street No. 6. There would be no escaping that final moment which he had eluded for years.

> He set down his coffee cup,
> The policeman said, 'Your time is up.'

Rudian really believed the moment had come. This was the only explanation for the investigator's sympathetic look and his insistence that he should have one more coffee and then another. It was his last chance to drink coffee in this world and the investigator felt sorry for him.

As far as he could tell, the case was being closed. The line of investigation had totally changed. This suicide, once a message designed for royalist émigrés, was now linked to a personal matter of which he was better left ignorant.

Since when was it better for the culprit to be unaware of his own guilt?

You must know, he thought, as if he were looking down at himself in handcuffs. If you don't know, find out. Only you can find out.

Something like a fork of lightning, resembling a thought but faster, shot through his brain. It involved guilt and innocence, his own and the state's, and both were mixed with a sense of fate, in which kindness and cruelty were still undifferentiated and all these things were like sparks scattered from an invisible core beneath a volcanic fissure.

He failed to grasp what this meant, because the crack had barely opened before it closed again and the sparks paled to ash, as if compressing the cooling of years into an instant.

Yet he felt he knew this thing that he could not see, whose obscure outline lay beneath that crack. Something had emerged, and he wanted to say that this case was still not closed. They had given up, but he hadn't. There was an enigma, as the investigator had admitted at the beginning, and had now apparently forgotten.

It was that filthy coffee that had caused all this confusion in his mind. If they thought he was better off not knowing, this meant that he was the very person who should know.

Find out, he said to himself again. Even if they didn't want to go on, he mustn't give up.

His own lack of inner response frightened him. It was up to him, more than them, to discover the truth.

Now he addressed himself not as before, but more gently, as if to persuade himself with kindness.

Why did it have to be my book that was sent to her with my signature? Quietly, without fuss, one day in early summer. That's a Phantom, his guide had said, just before the evening air raid in Vietnam. It flew silently, like a ghost. Hence its name.

Thousands of girls were interned all over Albania, but his Phantom had sought out this one.

Be careful, his Vietnamese guide had said to him that same night as they got ready for bed in a remote province; there might be cobras.

Oh hell, he thought, and then reflected that it didn't matter. It was this Vietnamese coffee that had brought it all back.

A stray Phantom flying into Albania's Barren Mountain. That's enough, he said to himself.

'There's something that doesn't fit,' he said aloud.

He would not have been surprised to find that the investigator had since left, but he was still there.

'What did you say?'

'I said that there is a mystery here. Nothing can persuade me there isn't.'

The investigator took a deep breath.

'I don't think so.'

'You said so yourself a while back, at the Party Committee.'

'I know. But later, after the investigation . . .'

Rudian could hardly hear him.

'Without knowing, I've been the cause of a tragedy,' he said wearily.

'Better not to think of it that way. Asking too many questions won't do any good.'

'I understand. When I was in Vietnam two years ago, we had little air-raid shelters like manholes next to our beds. If the bombers came during the night, we could jump in half-asleep, but my guide, whether seriously or to tease me, said I should be careful. There might be a cobra inside.'

The investigator bit his lower lip. 'I'm sorry you took it that way,' he said. 'And there's no question of threatening you. Even if I wanted to, I couldn't.'

'I understand. Let's drop this conversation.'

Again he felt exhausted, dulled. The single name of Caligula filled his brain for a short time.

'Perhaps it was a mistake for me to phone you,' he said very softly. 'I needed a person to talk to, and there was only you.'

'I understand.'

'As you may realise, in this story I have lost among other things the only other person I could talk to.'

'I'm sorry. I don't want to interfere, but if you mean the girl . . . I mean, your present girlfriend.'

'That's exactly who I mean,' Rudian said. 'I don't know what's happened.'

The investigator's eyes narrowed with concentration.

'I've simply lost touch with her. Usually she is the one to phone me.'

'I understand.'

'You see, I can't just whistle below the window of her aunt's apartment, like street kids do. She's living there temporarily, until school starts.'

'Of course not.'

You bastard, he chided himself before he opened his mouth again. You rotten bastard. So that was why he had sought out this meeting. He had hidden it so deviously from himself. Air raids in Vietnam, cobras, ersatz coffee, Fidel Castro's interminable speeches. In fact it was all about Migena's breasts.

Protest as much as you like, but you're the biggest bastard in the whole theatre, the whole of Tirana – the Venetian clock tower, mosque and statue of Skanderbeg included. You can't hide from your shame. You wanted the investigator to track down your lover, and that was all.

Incredible. He had not only thought it, but now he was unashamedly saying it. 'There's this one bloody telephone, just one for all the floors in the building, and you can imagine the use it gets. Quarrels, rumours, calls to the hospital, cake recipes.' The investigator listened thoughtfully. If Rudian wouldn't interpret it the wrong way, he was ready to help. It would be very simple for him. He would send a couple of his boys. They would know how to find the girl. They would know how to persuade her too. She would come looking for him herself, he'd soon see. As for tittle-tattle, he had no need to worry. These lads were used to keeping their mouths shut. They would think we were asking them to put her on his trail as an informer; you can imagine why.

So, Rudian thought, everything would happen just as he had imagined, when his suspicions were first awoken. An old-fashioned, hackneyed plot from the theatre.

'In the worst possible case,' the investigator continued, 'the lads might envy you a little. But that doesn't matter. You're used to that.'

And so they parted. A short time later Rudian wandered as if drunk past the National Bank. The idea struck him with the force of a revelation that this enigma was something bigger, beyond the province of the investigator and even the state.

8

Act Two. The edge of a marsh. On the bank, three feet from the water, the lifeless body of a partisan. To the right, down- stage, a desk. Two men sitting on chairs, files in front of them. A third man opposite them, apparently under interrogation.

RUDIAN STEFA leafed through the typed pages with irritation. He had been sure that the trouble began in the second half of the act, immediately after the ghost appeared, but it struck him now that the entire act was open to criticism.

Prompted by new rumours emanating from the Artis- tic Board, Rudian had spent the last two days reviewing the second act to identify what the focus of the criticism might be. He tried to imagine not only what the members of the Board had said but also their facial expressions. His imagination preferred to dwell on the beautiful face of the only actress on the Board. He knew that she was grieved at the way he had been treated, and her distress, about which he had been fully informed, was his sole consolation.

How could he make it clear to the audience that two different time frames were represented on the stage? The first was 1943, with the body of the murdered partisan beside the marsh, and the other was five years later, when a Party Commission was investigating covert assassinations. He conceded to his critics that there was a problem here. He and the producer would try to find the clearest solution, such as a sign inscribed in black and white: *February 1948. Commission to investigate the crimes of Koçi Xoxe, committed under Yugoslav pressure.* If this was thought to be too stark, too epic and Brechtian, they might add another sign with a quotation from the big chief: *The Party seeks the truth about these murders.*

If only that were all, Rudian sighed. There was sadness in the actress's eyes. Somebody had once said that sadness gave her eyes the beauty of stars. But this was scant comfort.

He began reading the text aloud to gauge better the impression it might create.

COMMISSION MEMBER 1 (*turning to the* DEFENDANT): You face charges relating to the murder of the partisan Robert K. in October 1943, at the place known as the Cuckoo's Field. Explain yourself.

DEFENDANT: It wasn't murder. I'm not a murderer. I was carrying out the sentence of the partisan court.

COMMISSION MEMBER 2: The reason for this sentence?

DEFENDANT (*hesitantly*): Inconsistency. Arrogance. Ridiculing his comrades . . .

COMMISSION MEMBERS (*almost in chorus*): Rather strange grounds.

Then the dialogue flowed smoothly:

You think that's an unusual accusation?

It didn't seem so at the time. Besides, he didn't mend his ways. He continued with his sarcasm.

Even after being sentenced?

Yes. It sounds incredible: a man sentenced to death, still sarcastic.

About what – death?

No, his own comrades.

I see, his own comrades. But what sort of court was this, which he wasn't scared of? Did he know that it had sentenced him to death?

Of course he knew.

And he still persisted in ridiculing it? But who witnessed his ridicule and how – wasn't he in a cell, handcuffed?

No, cells and handcuffs were bourgeois methods.

But he must have been confined in some cowshed, tied with rope.

No.

So he was free?

Yes.

And he was in a position to make fun of the court? Was the sentence a real death penalty – rather than symbolic, a moral reprimand?

Of course it was.

So he was going to be executed.

Precisely. First there were two other partisans who were supposed to kill him, but they couldn't.

Why not? What was stopping them?

He was still behaving in the same way.

So they couldn't kill him because he was making fun of them?

Evidently.

So he could be killed when he realised that he was going to be killed? In other words, when he stopped ridiculing his comrades and got ready for his own death?

(*The* DEFENDANT *remains silent.*)

This entire scene would have seemed beyond belief to Rudian if he hadn't found it in one of the Commission's files.

But perhaps the members of the Artistic Board had taken less notice of the scene's grotesque aspect, because at this moment the ghost appeared.

He had expected some of them to take fright at the ghost. What's this ghost doing here? Is this socialist realism or *Hamlet*? Others would have tried to stand up for him:

after all, ghosts weren't Shakespeare's invention or even Seneca's. All these things came from the people.

This defence seemed to him a good start, but still he couldn't rid his mind of the question of the ghost's presence. The answer flashed through his mind just before midnight as he was preparing for bed. It was a master-stroke of overriding arrogance that rendered insignificant all the events of the last few days: his summons to the Party Committee, his idle mornings, his Vietnamese–Cuban road to Calvary through the cafés of Tirana, and even Migena and her tears.

No dramatist had dared to make such an alteration to the figure of the ghost in thousands of years. It was not a superficial change – like making the ghost half vapor-ous and half real, or putting him in a dinner jacket and a gas mask – it was an essential reconception. His ghost would be dual-natured, if one could use such a term: a being or device not simply in possession of two minds or programmed in two ways, but with two ways of relating to others. For instance, in the scene where the shooter was interrogated by the commission and the body of the partisan on the bank of the marsh stood up and turned into a ghost, the ghost's conversation with the commission would be inaudible to the man who had killed him, and the words he exchanged with his killer would not be heard by the commission.

The dual-natured ghost, although present in a single reality, in fact acted in two dimensions, which did not overlap in any way. To make this more obvious on the stage, the ghost would be blue when he communicated with the killer, and another colour, violet or white, when he talked to the commission.

The part of the manuscript where the ghost appeared was covered with annotations. Only the beginning would stand: *The partisan's body slowly stands up from the place where it has been lying and comes forward to testify.*

Rudian made a revision: *The* GHOST, *lit in violet or white, comes forward.*

COMMISSION MEMBER 1: Robert K., you were killed by a bullet in the back of the head on the twenty-ninth of October 1943 at the place known as the Cuckoo's Field, on the bank of a marsh that has no name. Why were you sentenced by the partisan court?

GHOST: I was not sentenced by any partisan court. I was murdered by the man before you now, who shot me in the back of the head.

(*The* DEFENDANT *sits motionless, clearly not hearing anything of what is being said. He sees only the heads of the two commission members staring into empty space.*)

COMMISSION MEMBER 2: The defendant says you were condemned to death and he was carrying out the sentence of the partisan court. He says that you were sentenced for ridiculing your comrades, and that you continued to do this even after you were sentenced.

GHOST: I knew nothing of a death sentence. It is pure invention. I knew nothing about it. I wasn't ridiculing anybody. These people only thought I was.

(*The* GHOST *changes colour to blue. Just as he was invisible to the suspected killer when he spoke to the commission, now he is invisible to the commission when he speaks to the* DEFENDANT.)

GHOST: What was that tale about a partisan court? You know perfectly well there was no such thing.

DEFENDANT: There was a decision that you had to die.

GHOST: Why? Who said so? What had I done wrong?

DEFENDANT: You don't need to know.

GHOST: In any court, a defendant at least has the right to know why he's being sentenced.

DEFENDANT: What difference does it make? Everybody who remembers the case is dead except me. Nobody will listen to you.

GHOST: How can you be so sure?

DEFENDANT: You're getting above yourself. As always.

GHOST: I should at least know why. I was nineteen years old. Why did I have to die?

DEFENDANT: Better if you don't know.

(*The* GHOST *steps back towards the edge of the marsh, moves close to the partisan's body, and bends down to enter it.*)

COMMISSION MEMBER 1 (*to the* DEFENDANT): Then? What happened then?

DEFENDANT: Then we both set off to the town, the condemned man and I.

COMMISSION MEMBER 1: Why?

DEFENDANT: To carry out the sentence.

COMMISSION MEMBER 1: Why not in some clearing nearby? Behind some bushes? Behind a knoll? That's where people were usually shot.

DEFENDANT: I don't know. That's what had been decided.

COMMISSION MEMBER 2: Was the convicted man tied up?

DEFENDANT: No. The comrades trusted me.

COMMISSION MEMBER 1: Where had it been decided that he would be killed? In other words, who was going to decide on the place, you or him?

DEFENDANT: I was going to.

COMMISSION MEMBER 2: And then? What happened next? Go on.

DEFENDANT: Along the way I began to feel sorry for him. Regardless of what he'd done, we had been comrades-in-arms. I wanted to say to him, Run off, you're free. But at that very moment he turned his gun on me.

COMMISSION MEMBER 2: What? He was armed? Not only were his hands free, but he had a gun?

DEFENDANT: It was the custom in those days. Nobody's gun was ever taken away. We'll die with guns in our hands, that's what we used to say.

COMMISSION MEMBER 2: How strange . . . And then? Go on.

DEFENDANT: He pressed his gun in my back and marched me on. To the edge of the marsh. Night was falling. You could see the lights of the city, but very far away.

COMMISSION MEMBER 2: And then?

DEFENDANT: These lights confused him. And I took my chance and killed him.

COMMISSION MEMBER 1: Killing in self-defence. That's what you said before.

DEFENDANT: Yes.

COMMISSION MEMBER 1: Killing in self-defence. In the back of the neck . . .

(*At the edge of the marsh, the* GHOST *rises from the partisan's body, as if leaving its lair. It stands up and comes closer. It is violet in colour.*)

COMMISSION MEMBER 2: When did you realise that you had been sentenced to death?

GHOST: I never did.

COMMISSION MEMBER 2: You must have noticed something. A hostile attitude, some sort of aversion.

GHOST: That's true. Now and then there was something like that. But it came and went.

COMMISSION MEMBER 2: Did you have arguments, differences of opinion?

GHOST: Yes. They thought I was arrogant, temperamental, a typical city boy. For instance, we had different views about love. They disapproved of it. At least until the liberation. That's what they said.

COMMISSION MEMBER 1: And then? Why did you both set off for the city?

GHOST: That's what had been decided. We were told we were on a mission and that we would be briefed later.

COMMISSION MEMBER 1: Who gave the order for you to leave?

GHOST: The deputy commissar.

COMMISSION MEMBER 2: I see . . . Did he give you any final instructions?

GHOST: As far as I remember, he said something half-jokingly about reconciliation. Something about this mission bringing us closer together.

COMMISSION MEMBER 2: I see.

COMMISSION MEMBER 1: Did you talk along the way? Did you become closer, as the deputy commissar suggested, or did you have more serious disagreements?

GHOST: Neither of those things. We spent most of our journey in silence.

COMMISSION MEMBER 2: And then?

GHOST (*nodding towards the edge of the marsh*): Then we reached this spot. Dusk was falling. You could see the city lights in the distance. I hadn't seen them for such a long time. I stopped dead, and I felt terrible . . . homesickness. For him, apparently, they had the opposite effect. As I was standing there, he shot me in the back of the neck with his revolver.

(*The commission members talk among themselves and ask the* DEFENDANT *to go outside. The* GHOST *also moves back to the edge of the marsh.*)

COMMISSION MEMBER 1 (*leafing through the file*): Nothing new. This is the third time his file has been reviewed and we're still at square one.

COMMISSION MEMBER 2: Of course, whenever this case was reopened before, orders came immediately to close it again. Now we have firm instructions. Because it involves the Yugoslavs, there's no going back. Stalin's orders.

COMMISSION MEMBER 1: I don't believe it. The murderer still feels strong. He has his supporters and defenders.

COMMISSION MEMBER 2: You think?

COMMISSION MEMBER 1: I found in the file the letter he sent to the Central Committee two years ago. He says that the Party expelled him, but he remains as loyal to it as ever.

COMMISSION MEMBER 2: I know. Because of this letter, a young playwright wrote a hopelessly naive drama called *The Party's Faithful Dog*. And who do you think was punished for it? The dog? No way. The playwright. Eighteen years in prison.

COMMISSION MEMBER 1: That's what I expected.

(*They summon the* DEFENDANT *again.*)

COMMISSION MEMBER 1: I'm asking you for the last time . . .

(*The* GHOST *steps forward once more, this time blue.*)

GHOST: You hope you'll be let off this time too. It looks like they will sort it out for you. You're one of us, they will say. We look after each other.

DEFENDANT: Of course not.

GHOST: Do what you like, it's up to you. I just want to know, for the last time, why did you kill me?

DEFENDANT: I told you already: it's better if you don't know.

GHOST: I don't want to keep hearing that.

DEFENDANT: Is that a threat? I've seen so many like you. You're nothing. Nothing will come of nothing. Nothing ever—

GHOST: Answer my question. I'm asking you as a . . . I'm asking you as a . . . I'm not a man so I can't say as a man. But I'm asking you as a spirit, the soul of—

DEFENDANT: It's no use. I know how you suffer, and the grave won't hold you, so you keep appearing in different colours, but it's no use. You won't achieve anything. Each time, you just make your suffering worse.

GHOST: Who knows? One day you'll listen to me.

DEFENDANT: Ha ha, Get it into your head once and for all: even if one day I'm convicted, and it's proved that I killed you behind your back, one thing will never be revealed, the precise thing you are asking – the reason why.

GHOST: It will come out one day.

DEFENDANT: Never. Men cover up their business, like cats. Books, doctrines, nonsense about how leftism is an infantile disorder, and how you become right wing as you grow old . . . all these things cover up the truth.

GHOST: That's not so.

(*A frightening fork of lightning runs through the* GHOST'S *blue.*)

DEFENDANT: What was that?

GHOST: You shot me when you saw the lights of the city. Shortly beforehand, you were softening, but when you saw them, you went crazy.

DEFENDANT (*muttering, in agitation*): How do you know that?

GHOST: Death gives us our own venom. (*Another, even more frightening fork of lightning.*) Those lights revived all your old anger, which I noticed as soon as I arrived at the unit. From your very first words, when you said, Hey, high school boy, let's see how you turn out.

DEFENDANT: See, this is an important clue for us.

(A third fork of lightning.)

GHOST: No, it runs deeper than that. No girls ever looked sweetly at you. That's why you and all your sort were against love.

DEFENDANT: We had taken to the hills to fight, not for love.

GHOST: You did not like love, because love did not care for you. And you blamed me. Years have passed, and the war ended long ago, but still you have never felt the gentle touch of a woman.

DEFENDANT: Shut your mouth, corpse!

GHOST: You can make a new career. They might proclaim you a hero or a dissident. But still no woman will want to bring her neck close to yours. And still you will blame me for it.

DEFENDANT: Thing of darkness, go back to where you came from!

GHOST: That is the reason. Neither Marx nor Bakunin nor Plutarch discovered it. Nor Adam Smith, nor Berdyaev. That is the dark heart of the matter, as they say in Albanian. Envy.

DEFENDANT: Nonsense – empty words, just as you don't exist. I won. In the end, I shot you in the head.

The GHOST remains silent. Accepting defeat, the GHOST lowers his head and performs the ritual motions of surrender, re-entering the body on the edge of the marsh.

He had been looking at the written pages for a long time, almost in surprise, as if they were not his own. He was so tired he could barely distinguish the letters. Only the black lines through the parts to be cut were still clear. A great zigzag 'Z' resembled the symbol for electricity on a warning sign: *Danger!*

He couldn't take his eyes off it. This zigzag had less to do with the ghost than with himself. Instead of suggesting continuity, it represented the opposite, a fracture.

Even before, when he had thought of this scene, he had sensed there would be a snag. He had hoped that, as at other times, the knot would loosen itself, but this had not happened. He faced a barrier of mist, thicker than any curtain.

He had sat for hours on end in front of his plans for the scene. His notes, phrases, words, sketches, and the symbols that only he understood, became more and more complicated and he could not see past them.

Here was the precipice. A miracle or a disaster. What wings, what helicopter would carry him to the other side?

Sometimes, especially while he slept at night and everything became gentler and blurred, it seemed to him that the intangible was within his grasp. It was so close to him, and he only needed a moment to reach out and touch it, but then, at this very point, at the zigzag warning sign, his mind would seize up, as if in plaster. Stalled, and in a panic at the cost an attempt to break through would entail, he found he could only free himself by opening his eyes.

This had happened to him at the end of the ghost's scene. The zigzag sign had suggested a way out. Unconsciously, he had scrawled only a 'Z', like a road sign before dangerous bends. But unlike the ghost's two colours, this zigzag had proved a stubborn obstacle. A chill message from other worlds perhaps, alien to all forms of human understanding.

'This is impossible,' he confessed in a quiet voice; he could not tell to whom: a woman, a priest, or some sort of crowd consciousness.

The organs of the state were mysterious enough. Yet even beyond them, thick fog surrounded him on all sides. He could not tell from where he had to seek permission, if permission were necessary for every discovery or innovation in art.

His mind automatically returned to the parallel kingdom of sleep. Throughout those past two days he had kept thinking of the story of Orpheus, as if this old myth had collided with the planet and sprinkled everything with its glittering dust. Only one person was able to put to sleep Cerberus, the most famous of dogs, which guarded the gate of hell.

And it was not hard to imagine the rotor blades of the helicopters that were meant to spread sleep over Tehran, in order to free the hostages held there, not in the time of King Xerxes but in 1980. The helicopters with the US markings on their tails could make no headway through the sandstorm. The pilots gulped. It was impossible to go on. The rescue mission was failing. Of course it was going to fail, muttered the colonels who had opposed it. How could the idea for a twentieth-century military operation be drawn from an ancient myth?

The metal crates with their cargo of sleep scraped against each other as the helicopters swayed above the Iranian desert. Nobody knew what form this sedative substance took, whether powder, frozen granules resembling hailstones, or simply bullets.

Legend does not suggest that any other means apart from song enabled Orpheus to pacify the terrifying dog of hell. Still less is known about how this great city of Tehran, with its ayatollahs and mosques, was to be put to sleep. One could imagine that the training period must have been long.

And could something similar be done over the lowland plains of Albania? Putting to sleep the railways, cotton fields, farms, police stations, the barbed wire, the guards with their dogs? Orpheus too had prepared himself in utmost secrecy. Nothing was known about his training, apart from an adjustment he made to his lyre, increasing the number of strings from seven to nine. At first this was seen as a simple matter, but later it came to be seen as the greatest innovation for centuries.

Rudian Stefa, as so often when everyday events carried him into higher spheres, imagined the rumour spreading around Olympus. This musician had been extremely famous, so it was likely that the news of his recent invention was recorded in Olympian history. We all love Orpheus, Zeus had supposedly said, but still we can't permit him things we don't allow anybody else. Especially as he hasn't made clear why he needs those two extra strings. Perhaps I have old-fashioned tastes, but I think all our ears are accustomed to the old seven-stringed lyre.

To his left, Prometheus sat indifferent. He could not be expected to do anything but approve every gesture of rebellion. Surprisingly, it was the usually moderate Apollo who came out in the artist's defence, and with such passion that he not only supported the innovation but went further and asked that the number of muses be increased from seven to nine, to match.

The already-fraught debate became increasingly bitter. Artists' whims, said the anti-Orpheans. They want two more strings today, and who knows what half-baked ideas they'll come up with next. They should at least explain themselves, the god of war interrupted. It's perfectly clear when we look at new kinds of weapons. Do we want spears two inches or twelve inches longer, to get a better stab at the enemy? We don't go in for sophistry.

There were shouts for and against. Leave the artists to their work. No, if we do that it will be a disaster, like in the last century.

Zeus, inclined to vacillate on that day, postponed any decision. He was apparently aware of something the others were not.

As always, Rudian Stefa said to himself. Every tyrant has special knowledge.

He looked at the calendar on the wall. Three days had passed since his meeting with the investigator in the Café Flora. Today was the fourth. Migena had still not appeared.

Three days, today is the fourth, he repeated to himself. He was surprised not to feel any impatience.

9

S HE PHONED at last the next day, late in the afternoon.
Her voice was the same as before, soft, wreathed in
breath. 'It's me.' 'Yes,' he said. He wanted to say something
different, but the words had swirled round his mind as if
carried by a great gust of wind, and had come out in the
little frozen lump of this 'yes'. After a pause the girl said,
'I'd like to come over. May I?'

A muffled calm settled on his entire being. Of course, he
thought instantly, convinced that the girl would read his
thoughts faster than he could utter them. 'Of course,' he
said aloud. 'Come now.' The feeling of reassurance swept
over him so quickly that he realised he had been expecting
her to say something awful.

He imagined her arriving in her delicate high heels, and
the word 'darling', which he had so missed, at last bringing
him liberation.

He waited for her as he used to, pacing the corridor, and
as before, he discovered the little sounds that he usually
overlooked: water flowing through pipes in the building,
doors creaking for no reason, distant rasping noises, human voices.

The unmistakable click of her steps finally came.

They embraced without a word. Their arms tightened round each other, and when they couldn't hold each other any more closely she whispered in his ear, 'I'm sorry.'

Her cheeks were wet with tears, but her crying was not the same as before. Still half-embracing, they entered his study, where the last sunlight of the morning fell sometimes on the grip in her hair and sometimes on the names of his books. Fitzgerald. *Toponyms*. Nobody had moved them and the ill-omened landscape was still there: the Evil Gorge, Zeka's Field, Brigands' Gulch. The Three Crosses with the little shrine beyond them. Then the shrieks of the writer's demented wife, the echo of the rumbling avalanches in the Swiss mountains, and the luxurious sanatoriums.

She looked sidelong at the shelves as if searching for the scene of the disaster. 'I'm sorry,' she said again and, without waiting for him to ask why, went on to explain that it had been quite impossible for her to tell him that 'Linda B.' was interned. She hadn't slept for weeks, unable to decide what to do, especially after the inscribed book became so important.

Her words were mysterious. Perhaps this was all to the good, he thought, and they would understand each other better in this mist. 'Darling, have I caused you trouble?' she said between two caresses, and he replied in words so useless he forgot them instantly. He was used to it, meaning he was used to trouble, and he had been thinking of her. He wanted to ask if they had summoned her to the

Investigator's Office, but the question seemed premature. He did not need to tell her about his own summons to the Party Committee, and especially not about his meeting with the investigator in the Café Flora. He did not want to know how the two boys from the Investigator's Office had tracked her down in order to send her to him. He was sure that the two must have joked with each other over a beer late one afternoon about the pretty girl they were sending to this writer. That while he was having his fun with her in bed he would never dream she was the one who was springing the trap on him.

The thought of their laughter sparked the anger he needed to control himself. Cautiously, he asked if she had received any kind of summons, perhaps from an investigator.

She replied quietly that she had been interviewed once, but she didn't know which office they belonged to. They had come to her home and asked her about the book, in front of her father. That was the first and last time.

'Aha,' he said, involuntarily. More or less the same as in his case, he thought. The cautious questioning they do with favoured people.

She stroked his neck and rested her head against his chest.

'I didn't betray you,' she said very softly.

Rudian moved his shoulders, as if to say: How could you possibly betray me? With startling suddenness he pictured *Doctor Zhivago*, Koestler's *Darkness at Noon*, and Heidegger's trap, lined up alongside *Toponyms*. The Brigands' Well, Mark Marku's Fields, the Evil Ambush.

He smiled bitterly. As the investigator had explained to him, he could not be betrayed. Great acts of treason were not betrayed by others, they were invented.

Almost whispering, she told him that they had asked her about his books too, but only in passing. The one thing they had wanted to know was whether he had been aware before of Linda and her internment, or whether she, Migena, had instigated everything.

He listened in confusion, because he was thinking of something else. He took a deep breath and thought of looking at her eyes when he asked his next question, but decided against it. Finally he ventured the question cautiously and in a very quiet voice, holding his head to one side so that her eyes were invisible to him.

Migena clung to him, motionless and without hope.

Say something, he thought, surprised by a cold, dead anger within him, of the kind one might catch in one's own reflection in a mirror.

'Tell me,' he said out loud. 'I asked you about Linda. Did they interrogate her?'

'I don't know what to say,' the girl replied. 'I think they did.'

Of course. They handled us two with great care. But what did they do to Linda?

This was more or less what he said to her, but to his surprise Migena shook her head.

'They didn't harm her? Are you sure?' he asked. In Albania, investigators' offices had blood on the floor. How could he explain that to her?

Migena was certain. She had met Linda that same afternoon when the investigators had gone to her house. Linda said that they had questioned her but she didn't go into details. That was her way, to avoid anything to do with politics.

'Perhaps she didn't want to say how horrible it had been,' Rudian said.

'No,' Migena said. 'She didn't give the least hint of the kind of thing you're imagining.'

'How strange,' Rudian said. 'I don't understand this.'

'Believe me,' Migena said sweetly, bringing her head close to his shoulder.

In a low murmur she told him how, over the next few days, they had talked again about Linda's interview. It had concentrated entirely on the book and on Rudian himself. Did she know him or not? Had they exchanged letters or messages? That was all.

Rudian was relieved. It seemed that Linda's suicide had nothing to do with the book.

He sensed that Migena wanted to say something more. In the same sweet voice she described how Linda was not only undaunted by her interview but, incredibly, had seemed excited by it. It was a shock, but a pleasant one. The dreamy glow that regularly illuminated Linda's eyes increased. As they listed their friends to work out which of them, perhaps Natasha Hysa or Flora Dulaku, might have seen the book, she had seemed distracted and unconcerned.

'You won't believe it, but she told me that they hadn't upset her at all, and she even wanted them to question her again.'

He frowned.

'Are you serious?'

Migena nodded, deepening the furrows of suspicion on her brow.

'It wasn't a good sign,' she said in a muffled voice.

Again, their eyes did not meet.

It was not easy to explain. A girl with a rounded character like Linda had still felt unfulfilled. A couple of flirtations or semi-flirtations with boys at school had been disappointing. This was the first time she had, as you might put it, acquired a story.

'What kind of story?' he butted in. 'How can something like this be called a story?'

She begged him not to interrupt her. For Linda it was more than a love story. It was a romance involving Rudian Stefa, the well-known playwright. Linda had been following him for at least two years – reviews in the papers, on the news, television interviews – dreaming of meeting him and getting to know him, while aware that this was impossible. Suddenly she had a direct connection with her adored playwright. The investigators had asked: Have you ever met him? Why did he write 'a souvenir from the author'? The word 'souvenir' implies that something has happened that should be remembered. What are your feelings for him? What are his feelings? What does 'Linda B.' mean? You said that it's a reference to a poem by Migjeni addressed to 'Miss B.'

He listened to her gentle voice, his face motionless.

'How can you not understand?' She broke off. 'This story was about you! You must see that . . . About you! It was the only way she could get . . . involved with you.'

'Don't be upset,' he said. 'I'm aware of that and I understand it very well. It happens often.'

'No,' she said. 'I've heard the stories about fans and how they behave. This was different. Can't you see that Linda really was different?'

'I do see that,' he said. 'Maybe better than you.'

Offended, she turned to the window. The street and the trees in the small park beyond had never looked so remote.

'Perhaps I can see why you can't grasp the whole situation,' she said, turning back. 'You still don't know the most important thing.'

Something else, Rudian said to himself. A wave of anger swelled inside him. In this story he was always the ignorant one. There was no end to it.

'And what might that be?' he asked icily.

'Don't look like that. You don't know that she . . . desired you.'

'We talked about that.'

'No, we didn't. She wasn't just an admirer of yours. She loved you in the full sense of the word – do you understand? She wanted to meet you, to touch you, to kiss you, to do everything. Now do you understand?'

His frown deepened. He shook his head. No, he thought. This was not natural. It was a misunderstanding. His. Hers.

Migena went on with her story. Linda had been obsessed with him for two years. She made no secret of it. When Migena had brought her the inscribed book, her cup was overflowing. She was totally overcome with emotion.

Rudian noticed Migena's pained expression when he interrupted her to say his thoughts aloud.

She studied him incredulously.

'You don't like it? How strange . . . Anybody else would be pleased.'

Oh hell. How to explain to her that this was not a quirk of his? Like most men he was vain enough to feel pleased that women desired him. But not in Linda's case.

'Not at all,' he said.

He was becoming confused. This had been happening more and more frequently. Sometimes his mind would clear only to grow dim again. It was not merely male vanity that discomposed him, but something else mixed in with it. Perhaps he wanted to shirk responsibility for all that had taken place and for the illusion of himself he had recklessly conjured up.

Feverishly he began talking about these things and found himself repeating familiar phrases. All of this was unnatural. He wished none of it were true, and hoped to persuade Migena so too.

The girl could barely follow him. At the first opportunity she interrupted and turned the conversation back to his inscribed book. She recalled the warm June evening. How Linda's hands had trembled when she had received it. Migena had thought she was making her friend happy.

Her voice faltered with emotion, and he gently touched her hair. The girl did not manage to say that instead of happiness she had brought her tragedy, but Rudian understood. Again, it was my fault, he thought. However you looked at it, he was to blame.

She was in a kind of ecstasy, Migena continued. She had been the prettiest girl in school, yet the more beautiful she grew, the more people gave her strange looks, as if to say: What's the point? Where can you go? Then came those two or three hectic weeks that were so difficult, with his inscribed book, her interrogation, the breast scan, and the evening of their farewell ball, one after another.

'Breast scan?' he interrupted. 'Did you say breast scan, or didn't I hear you right?'

Migena didn't lift her eyes.

'That's what I said – breast scan.'

He listened to her breathing and then his own.

'A breast scan, which women have when there's a suspicion of—'

'Exactly,' she said. 'But not so fast—'

'What do you mean, not so fast? Why not? Do you know what you're saying?'

'Don't be offensive.'

'You never mentioned this to me. Why do you hide everything? Why can't you talk honestly?'

'I talk the way I know. Not everybody is a playwright like you.'

What a ridiculous thing to say, he thought. He glanced involuntarily at what he had come to think of as his place of punishment – his bookshelves, where last time he'd seized her by the hair. The Cuckoo's Path was still there. The Bandit's Grave, the Wedding-Guests' Ambush and the Dark Ravine. Zelda Fitzgerald's screams in luxurious asylums.

His nerves had been frayed and the mention of a breast scan had only increased his distress. But this scan changed everything connected to the suicide. An unfavourable result could have led to suicidal thoughts. Why hadn't she told him and released him from blame? He stroked her hair and then her neck. She touched his hand with hers.

'It's true. I'm mixed up,' she said. 'Perhaps later when I'm calmer . . .'

Later, he thought. Of course, naked in his warm bed, everything would be easier.

Reading his mind she said, 'We won't make love, we won't . . .'

Rudian acquiesced in silence. He couldn't tell why, but he sensed that it had to be like this. It was the only way.

'At least not today,' she went on. He kissed her neck as a sign of understanding before they sat down on the sofa. 'This story's not easy for me to explain,' she said. 'It's even more complicated.'

She asked him to be patient and he gave her his promise.

Dusk was falling and muffled sounds came from the street.

So the scan was the reason, he thought. Why hadn't she said so?

The lights of the few cars, silent bloodless reptiles, shone on the walls of the apartment.

'It was all about getting to Tirana,' Migena said vaguely, as if talking to herself.

She continued in a monotonous voice, as if trying to lull him to sleep. She had never known anyone to love, with such wild intensity, a city they had never seen. It occurred to Rudian that this is how you love cities that you have no hope of visiting, like Dante's Florence, but he was scared of interrupting.

Migena had learned from Linda the regulations governing internment: Linda had to report to the police at a certain time every afternoon. There were sanctions for absconding: a statutory punishment for visiting a nearby town; double for cities further away; and much more for the capital city – life imprisonment or execution.

Migena would sometimes come to Tirana with her father or uncle. When she returned, Linda would bombard her with endless questions. Were the almond trees in bloom in the park opposite the Dajti Hotel? What first nights had there been at the theatre? What were girls wearing that season? She knew Tirana better than its inhabitants. From documentaries, the television news and hearsay, she knew the squares, cinemas, cafés. Sometimes she would ask impossible questions. How long did it take to walk from the clock tower to Dibra Street, which they called Broadway? And what about the boys who hung around the pavements – had she seen the Broadway lads, as they were known? Between the main boulevard and Elbasan Street there were some side streets with beautiful villas. Had she ever gone that way? What about the advertisements at the main theatre, were they lit up for first nights? What about the atmosphere at the Café Flora? Of course girls went there with their boyfriends, didn't they? From a distance, could you tell if they were flirting?

Migena had learned to become observant for Linda's sake. It was true that between the main boulevard and Elbasan Street there were fine villas from the thirties, with iron railings. After their expropriation, some had become foreign embassies. One of these villas must have belonged to Linda's family, but this was the kind of sensitive political issue that she never mentioned. As for what you might call 'society gossip', Migena had heard talk of a romance between N.F., the most recent Hamlet, and a young actress, not the one who played Ophelia, as people thought at first, but a younger and less famous understudy. She'd also vaguely heard something about a very beautiful young writer, fresh from the provinces.

'Sometimes I would embellish details – add lights, glass doors, tall buildings – so she wouldn't be disappointed. I knew that she wrote all this in her diary alongside impressions from her reading or from radio plays.'

Migena took a deep breath. She looked tired.

'Then something happened,' she said after a silence. 'You appeared on the stage. Perhaps you remember talking on television before the premiere of your play?'

During the lunch break at school, Linda had asked if she could come over in the evening to watch an interview with the playwright Rudian Stefa, announced on the radio. 'She often did this because we had a television and her family didn't. She came at the agreed time, looking as beautiful and serious as ever, her hair neatly combed, as if going out to a party. She followed carefully every word you said, watched every movement of your fingers, and noticed at one point your barely concealed irritation at the interviewer. The look on her face was almost one of awe, mixed with pain, or rather worry. When the interview was over, her eyes glistened and she said softly: He's different, in every way. It was not hard to see that her vision of Tirana needed a human being in it. You filled that gap.'

He managed to interrupt. That was exactly what he'd said to her earlier, about filling a gap. It was a coincidence, and nothing more. First she had yearned for Tirana, and then there was this gap to be filled by someone in the city such as, in this case, himself.

Migena continued as if she hadn't heard. Linda made no secret of the fact that she never stopped thinking about him. She dreamed about him, wrote about him in her diary. It was in those last days before graduation, in that atmosphere familiar to everybody: worry about university places, the pain of parting, and words left unsaid. Migena went to and from Tirana more often than ever before. She was almost certain to be accepted at the Art College, but even she shared the general excitement. Linda had nothing to look forward to. It was from one of these trips that Migena brought back his inscribed book. 'It was this that drove her totally out of her mind. Linda no longer concealed anything. She was not merely in love. She was totally infatuated with you. Her longing for you, for Tirana, her misery at not being able to go, and her pain at parting from me, all multiplied twofold, tenfold. The criticism of your play in the newspapers made everything worse. She dreamed of impossible things, of being close to you and consoling you whenever you were down. Her fever rose to such a pitch that I began to regret what I had done. I'd been so pleased to surprise her in this way, but with every day that passed, I became more convinced that I should never have brought her that book.

'Then came those three or four crazy weeks. My interview at the investigator's, my father's anxiety, and her interview, which instead of dampening her fantasies about you had the opposite effect. We never discovered who the spy was who told them about the book and we had little time to speculate. Events came on like a sequence of avalanches: the news of my scholarship to the Art College, but nothing for Linda, and the breast scan, immediately followed by the graduation ball.'

The shock lifted Rudian Stefa to his feet. He seized her arm, as if his hoarse shout of 'Wait!' were not enough.

Stop, he thought. You won't get away with it this time.

In vain the girl struggled to free her arm. She looked at Rudian as if he had gone crazy.

'Wait,' Rudian said again. 'This is the second time you've mentioned this breast scan without explaining anything.'

'What is there to explain?' she said in a chill voice.

'Was this a breast scan as I understand it, a suspicion of cancer in the breast, possibly deadly?

'Precisely,' she replied with the same coldness. 'For analysis. Possibly fatal.'

'Then why not finish the story?' Rudian cried. 'This scan explains everything. What do I need all the rest for? Why do I need the graduation ball? And all those fantasies about me? This scan explains why she died.'

Her eyes absorbed nothing and revealed nothing, as if cataracts had descended on them. Then, an ironic glitter of the kind Rudian could not bear crept into them.

Migena stood up.

'You won't let me,' she said. 'You're not helping me, you're stopping me from talking.'

'Me? Stopping you?'

'Yes, you. Can't you see I'm not ready? Don't you understand how hard this is for me?'

She hid her face in her hands, but her weeping, visible only in the movements of her shoulders, was even harder to endure.

'It's late. I'm going.'

'No.'

It seemed to him that time had run backwards to their last meeting in front of the bookshelves, before this horror began.

'What are you hiding from me?' he cried, as he had done back then.

He was surrounded by a void, and in this void, before his very eyes, something was happening with which he could not interfere.

The girl was walking towards the door of his apartment.

Don't go. These words ran through his mind, just as he recalled how he had seized her hair and dragged her back to Scott Fitzgerald, the Evil Ambush and Death Rock.

The clicking of her heels and her final 'goodnight' were cut off by the closing door.

Can't you see I'm not ready? he repeated to himself. Language of the theatre, he thought, but immediately he felt that he had treated her unfairly.

10

I T TOOK him a long time to shake off his grogginess. He'd slept in again. He knew it. At least spare him that irritating saying about it being the first sign of psychosis. He banished it from his mind but at a certain cost. Out of the rain and into the hailstorm. It was Wednesday, the day when the Artistic Board met. Couldn't he start the day with a different thought? But no, there it was, every Wednesday, ten o'clock, the bloody Board meeting. He imagined them taking their places at the long table, blowing on their cold hands, with the stove smoking away.

He rubbed his eyes and went to the door to fetch the post. An invitation to meet readers at the Porcelain Enterprise. A letter from the Writers' League: his request to extend his sabbatical had been refused. Electricity and water bills. For the first time in his life he read the figures, with simulated interest. Previous monthly reading: 014154 kW. Water for April to May: 37 leks. Why was he doing this? He set them aside for later.

He looked at the telephone with a faint hope that it might be broken and roughly lifted the receiver, but was disappointed to hear the dialling tone. Heap of junk. It worked when it shouldn't. It would have been Migena's only possible excuse for not calling: I tried so many times, but the line was down. Nothing from her for two days. Today was day three.

What the hell, he said to himself, his eyes darting round as if in search of something to get angry about.

He could predict almost word for word what his long-standing enemy R.B. would say: Cutting out that ghost is an absolute must, otherwise I'll vote against.

He looked at his watch. Perhaps this hadn't been said yet. As he shaved, he tried not to think about what the Board members were saying. Perhaps they were still dealing with the smoking stove.

For a little while he derived a certain pleasure from imagining them coughing and cursing the stove and the damp wood.

From nowhere, the idea came to him of inserting a Serb in the middle of Act Two. A Serbian villain would do the trick, along the lines of Dušan Mugoša, sent by the Yugoslavs to the Albanian partisans to plot secret murders. As always, inspiration excited him. He got dressed briskly, almost whistling with joy, but his elation subsided as suddenly as it had risen. He had remembered the thin, scratchy voice of the minister of culture. You playwrights, she would say, whenever you get stuck, you shove in an evil Serb to justify some ghastly scene.

What a witch, he said to himself. Her voice was all he needed on a day like this.

His psychiatrist had explained one evening that an inclination of the mind to dwell on unpleasant things or bad news is a sign of a pre-depressive state.

I know that, he had almost said aloud. Couldn't the doctor say anything else?

Nevertheless, he went to the phone and dialled the doctor's number.

His voice was as reassuring as ever. Was he suffering from anxiety again? Poor sleep, irritation? This was nothing to worry about. He could see him again if he wished. They could try a different tranquiliser. Whenever he wished. 'Next week, Wednesday for instance.' 'Wednesday? Well . . .' 'Or another day if you're busy.' 'Not at all, Wednesday would be ideal for me too.' 'Early evening perhaps.' 'Early evening is fine.' 'Six thirty, OK?'

The doctor had read his mind. Even if the decision about the play were postponed today, the question would be settled by next Wednesday for certain. It was the best possible day for an appointment.

Incorrigible, he thought. Always anticipating the worst, and then complaining when things didn't turn out as expected. 'Can you hear me, Doctor? Yes, yes. I don't know what was wrong with the line. I wanted to say something else, but not about myself. It's about a young woman, in our family . . . I wanted to say . . . after an unfavourable breast scan, is there a danger that, out of despair . . . she might harm herself?'

From the other end of the wire, the doctor's voice lost its exuberance. Of course it couldn't be ruled out. It depended on the circumstances, and especially the character of the patient. 'I understand,' said Rudian. 'She's a young woman, extraordinarily beautiful—' 'That doesn't make it easier for her,' the doctor interrupted. 'On the contrary—' 'What do you mean, on the contrary? Do you mean that beautiful women are more prone to suicide?' 'That could be true,' the doctor said, 'but it's more complicated than that.'

Rudian apologised. 'Six thirty then, on Wednesday,' he said, and replaced the receiver.

He paced his study, paused in front of his wall calendar, and circled Wednesday in red.

Two days, today is day three, he thought. For the umpteenth time he rehearsed what he would say to Migena. The ploy of not phoning was a familiar, always successful strategy: to get the better of your partner and make yourself desirable, and so on. But Migena was forgetting that they'd talked about this. She should have been aware that he knew this tactic very well, so that it not only didn't work on him, but had the opposite effect.

If only she would come, he thought. He was sure that half, if not all of his anger would evaporate.

His mind, in search of a peaceful haven, wandered again to that memorable day on Olympus when the gods talked of nothing but Orpheus' distress. Aside from the question of approving his innovation or not, there was another concern, of which Zeus alone was aware: the sickness of the young woman to whom the musician was engaged. She grew paler every day and was racked with pains throughout her body, especially in the chest. Nobody knew, not even Zeus, about the connection between her illness and the two additional strings on the lyre.

After Eurydice's death, the truth slowly seeped out. Orpheus was asking for something impossible: her return from beyond the grave. He began to employ his art, which he had so far used only to entertain and win celebrity, to extract consent for this difficult request. His task was to enchant with his singing the ministers of hell. His music had to move Hades himself. The blind god was indeed moved by the artist's voice, and just as much by the homage the artist paid to him. Artists were accustomed to the luxuries of Olympus and rarely paid any attention to hell. Yet Hades took no revenge for this indifference. On the contrary, he listened with the utmost appreciation, without demanding any of the favours that evil tongues expected he would want, such as hymns to hell or free concerts for the dead. Hades was not like that. He knew how to behave like a gentleman, even though what was being asked of him was not easy. No inhabitant of hell had ever left his realm. Yet Hades was sure that the obstacles, however serious, were not insuperable, except for the matter of Cerberus, the dog guarding the gate. The question was not whether the famous Orpheus would sing to a dog – he might be persuaded to do such a thing for Eurydice's sake – but would it have any effect? The dog was of an unknown breed and totally unresponsive to any intercession, human or divine.

Perhaps there is some hope, Orpheus said. He talked about the new feature he wished to introduce to his music with those celebrated two strings. Hades had heard something about it, but only vaguely. Orpheus had sensed that destiny would turn against him, and like a man casting round for a means of salvation, he had been looking for a new and unparalleled form of music.

What were the two new strings for? Why were they necessary? Now this riddle that had so preoccupied the curious minds of Olympus that summer would at last be solved.

Hades shook his head in disbelief. Cerberus the dog, which Orpheus hoped to tame with his song, would never in all eternity allow anybody to pass the gate. The only hope lay not in charming the beast, but in lulling him to sleep.

Orpheus was sure he could do it. Hades wished him luck, but explained to him one last condition. This was a compulsory bargain between Orpheus and Hades himself, or in other words with death. It was an apparently simple agreement, whose fulfilment depended entirely on Orpheus.

If it depends on me, I'll do it, however cruel it is, said Orpheus.

We'll see, said Hades, and in a few words outlined the deal.

The ring of the telephone came to him from a distance, sounding somehow uncanny. In slow motion, Rudian stood up, went to the phone and lifted the receiver. Then came the low female voice: 'It's me.'

Migena. A longing that he had never felt before enfolded him. He could not bear it. Did he say or only think the words 'I was waiting for you' or 'I was waiting for you, darling' or merely 'darling'?

He must have said something like that, because she replied, 'I want to come over, but . . . ' 'But what?' he said, his voice faint. 'Is there a problem?' 'I'm not alone, I'm together with Linda.' 'Oh, I see,' he said, less astonished by this than he should have been. 'So there are two of you.' 'Naturally,' said the girl's voice. How peculiar, he thought. From these words, from these thoughts even, something was missing. 'Could we both come, if possible?' Migena asked. 'Together? With Linda? Naturally.' Rudian used Migena's word even though he knew that it was the least appropriate choice at that moment. He wanted to ask if there was any hindrance, but the only reply was the hum of the interrupted phone line, as if he had said something wrong.

What have I done? he thought, and immediately woke up from his somnolent state. Oddly, he still felt sorry that he had not heard the reply. How had they received permission? How had they lulled to sleep the Ministry of Internal Affairs?

Sleep a while longer, he thought. But it was late morning now. He could keep his eyes shut for as long as he liked, but nothing would save him from wakefulness.

It is you who has to lull Cerberus to sleep, he said to himself. Everything was fraught with meaning and at the same time meaningless. They were both there – meaning and non-meaning – in the briefest coexistence imaginable. It was no use him crying for them to stay together a moment longer. The two separated, as one would expect, each to its own business.

Abhorring the vacuum left behind, his mind wandered back to the celebrated bargain. There had been a lot of discussion about it, as well as of the two extra strings. Was there or was there not a deal, and if there was, why was it being kept secret?

As expected, when the truth came out the rumours were stilled. There really was a deal, and like all classical bargains it was very simple. After sending Cerberus to sleep, Orpheus had to meet a single condition. While leaving hell, he must not turn round to look at his beloved, who would be following him. This was the essence: however intense his longing, however urgent his impatience, he must not turn his head. If he looked back, he would lose her. For all eternity.

To most of the Olympians, the deal seemed easy. He had only not to turn his head. The challenge should have been at least, say, to have his bride in his bed and not to touch her. There were muttered complaints everywhere about concessions made to artists while others got it in the neck for the slightest mistake. These continued until the news came that Orpheus had lost his chance. His beloved had called out to him with such tenderness that he had not been able to resist the temptation. There was some sympathy for him. Poor fellow, his love got the better of him. But some Olympians said: How feeble, the typical artistic type.

A third group of gods who rarely spoke up took a different view. They were convinced that the deal had been bogus. No Eurydice had been following Orpheus when he crossed over from hell. This turning of his head had been a diabolical trick. As long as she was unseen, Eurydice was supposedly there, and Orpheus won credit, but as soon as he turned to look at her, she melted away, and for this he was to blame. So, either way, there was nothing there and Orpheus lost.

But what if Orpheus had not fallen into the trap? asked one dissenting voice. If he had kept his side of the bargain and not turned his head, what would have happened then?

What would have happened? The moment would inevitably have come when he turned his head. The road was long, night would fall – apparently the deal didn't say for how long he shouldn't turn his head . . . Another way out might have been found.

The story might be called 'The Deception of Orpheus'. There was a reason why it was called humankind's darkest myth.

Rudian Stefa sat down on the sofa.

If only she would come, he said to himself again. The Evil Ambush. The Three Wells. That evening now seemed so far away. He wandered to the telephone again, without knowing why. He lifted the receiver and left everything to his fingers. The investigator's voice down the wire did not sound as friendly as before. It was polite but nothing more. There was no allusion, even obliquely, to their previous conversation. 'I just phoned you, for no reason,' Rudian said for the second time. The investigator thanked him, and finally mentioned their coffee. 'I would like us to have coffee together, but you can't imagine how busy we are these days.' Rudian hardly waited before banging down the receiver. What was all that for? He cursed under his breath. The bitch, what has she done to me? A few moments later the renewed ringing sounded alien, out of place. He picked up the receiver with the confidence of someone who at last has the right to speak his mind. But he was brought up short by words in a foreign language, apparently German, and his name, mispronounced strangely, in the middle of the flow. He replied in English, 'Yes,' and then recognised Albana's voice: 'My dear, how are you?'

She could hardly have chosen a worse time to call. 'Hello, can you hear me?' her voice continued. 'Yes, but the line's bad.' 'I can hear you fine.' 'But not this end.' 'Hello, how about now, is that better?' 'I don't know. This hellish handset.' 'Hello, are you well, my dear?' 'What?' 'I asked you, are you well?' 'I don't know, I can't hear.' 'Darling, it seems to me . . . What's the matter with you?' 'Nothing's the matter. Why should there be? How do you know I'm not well? How do you think I should be? Eh?'

For a moment there was silence. He could hear the woman's breathing, so the connection must have been in order.

'Did you get an answer about the play?' she asked hesitantly. 'Not yet,' he replied. 'Aha,' she said, to imply she understood the situation. 'Don't worry, darling, I thought as much . . . I had a bad feeling about it. I'd like to be with you at a time like this. But my internship has been extended by three weeks. I wanted to tell you.' 'Never mind, never mind,' he replied. At least the delayed answer about the play had come in useful for one thing – it was the best possible excuse for being tongue-tied on the phone. She wouldn't repeat her awkward question of whether there was anything wrong, which would force him to give a vacuous reply rather than admit that something irreparable had happened and he needed to recover his balance; that there was a ghost they were insisting on cutting from his last play, and a suspected tumour – no, not his, but someone else's – which was perhaps his fault.

He had rarely had such a conversation, where things he said aloud were interlaced and confused with things he had only thought, or half-said. Of course he needed her – the sweet anaesthetist who soothed away his pain, who brought him oblivion, not just because they whispered to one another in their moments of intimacy, but beyond this. He remembered these things, but there was something else, something sad. Several sad things had happened while she had been away. It was not just the apartment that had sunk into chaos, but his whole life. 'Perhaps we should have got married last summer,' he said. 'Do you think it's too late to get married now?' 'I didn't say that.' 'Don't start turning against the idea yourself. I've got enough on my hands with everybody else being against it. You're not well, Rudian. Tell me if you need me; I'm ready to drop this internship and come back.' 'No, don't say that.' Of course, he thought to himself, I'd like you to put me under, in the way you know best, at which you're so skilled, without the need for this internship in Austria, to put me to sleep for a long time, a very long time, but I'm afraid that no sedative can make me forget.

He had replaced the receiver long ago, but the conversation continued in his imagination.

Get outside as much as you can, the doctor had told him last time. If you haven't any reason to go out, invent one.

Well, he thought, he didn't need to invent excuses. He had a special reason, that neither the psychiatrist nor anyone else would ever know: Linda B. He felt he had already made an agreement with her, a strange agreement to show her, as if to a tourist, the Tirana of her dreams.

It was getting dark. As usual, he stared at the street for a few moments before going out. A jungle, he thought, with Vietnamese coffee. And only here and there, very rarely, an anaconda – that is, Brazilian coffee – instead of the cobra.

Sometimes, on those unforgettable Tirana evenings when the light of the moon and the fragrance of the lime trees grew stronger, Linda B. also underwent a transformation, from a tourist into his fiancée. She linked her arm in his, and both of them set words aside.

Their imagined conversation usually began in the city centre. From the National Bank to the Café Flora it was only a five- or six-minute walk. Really? I thought it was a bit further. It's the same name as that famous café in Paris, isn't it? Café de Flore. Exactly the same.

As they passed the Marionette Theatre she looked afraid and averted her eyes from a poster showing a masked puppet. For a moment he thought he understood the reason why, but his insight was vague, and the clue vanished at once.

A walk to the Writers' Club would take them past King Zog's former palace, or directly through the square with the ministry buildings.

He was often tempted to tell her more about the club during the sixties, when under their breath people called it the Petöfi Club, because of its counterpart in Budapest. But he decided against it. She was very young, and also under political suspicion. Passing the garden of the Academy of Sciences, they usually did not speak again until they had reached Caernarvon Street and the dark shadow cast by the National Library, which had previously been the princesses' palace. At this point he would ask 'Are you tired, darling?' and she, resting her head on his shoulder, would admit that even though she never thought that happiness could tire her, she did feel truly exhausted. But to him it seemed natural for a girl who had not walked for several days (twelve days, day thirteen today), or who, in other words, had lain still, like everyone under the earth.

They would turn back, and he would accompany her to the door of the Drini Hotel, in whose garden there had been dancing a long time ago. Here he would embrace her gently and he would return to his apartment. Luigj Gurakuqi Street was very close and he would extend his walk by going round the Opera House.

He did so on this evening too. On Barricade Street he paused as usual in front of the antique shop. They had taken the expensive rings out of the window, as they did every evening after the shop had closed.

The sound of singing in a protracted, nasal voice came from the Voza beer hall. Rudian stopped to make out the words.

> *The man who takes me for his wife*
> *Will have a star, not a woman, all his life.*

A few steps further on, he stopped to listen again.

He repeated the words to himself and shook his head. How strange.

Later, at almost midnight, when he opened the door of his apartment he felt paper rustling underneath it. He bent down to pick up the paper and recognised Migena's handwriting: *I phoned you twice. I'll phone again at ten o'clock tomorrow, M.*

II

H ER FACE seemed whiter. Her keen eyes, combined with her paleness, made her more desirable.

He drank a little brandy, then stared at the glass that he'd set down on the corner of the table in his study. Migena seemed to be trying to convey something to him. He looked at her smile, which should have been accompanied by words and appeared bereft without them. Rudian felt sure he knew what she was not saying. There was a rumour that a few days ago the Leader had issued another warning about the perils of foreign influences, citing the example of girls drinking brandy in the cafés of the capital city.

Waiting perhaps for nightfall, they spoke all the words they needed to say. Finally, in a very soft voice, so faint that if what he said annoyed her he might claim that he had not spoken but had only thought the reprehensible words, he asked, 'Shall we go next door?'

To his astonishment, she stood up without speaking and led the way into the bedroom. As he drew the curtains, she calmly undressed and with the same natural movements lay down on his bed.

They embraced for longer than they had ever done and made love without a word.

How easy this had been, he thought, without knowing exactly what 'this' was. He was stroking her breasts, but it occurred to him that he had still not uttered to her the words that should accompany his caresses.

He had rehearsed so many versions that he was sure that nothing but gibberish would come from his mouth. But the girl did not ask him what he meant. Perhaps she too was confused in her mind.

She listened to him attentively, before telling him that it was not as he imagined it.

'We both had breast scans,' she said after a moment. 'In fact, it was at first not for Linda's sake, but mine.'

He tried to remain calm.

'So it was you,' he said. 'I thought the opposite . . . I thought it was her . . . But it was you and not her who noticed the signs, who suspected . . . my darling.'

His hand instinctively stroked her breasts more slowly, as if fearful of finding a lump.

'My darling,' he whispered in her ear. 'When you just said you both did it, I thought it was her who felt the need, and you helped her.'

The girl's silence suggested only doubt.

'It's a bit more complicated,' she whispered in his ear. 'At first it really was for me, but then she wanted to do it too.'

'I see, so she had the same symptoms.'

'Wait, slow down. At first it wasn't a question of symptoms or suspicions. She was just going to accompany me to the hospital. Then she had the idea of having a scan, but there was no way she could do it without me.'

'I see, I can imagine that – in her situation.'

Migena shook her head.

'Perhaps you think she didn't have the right to treatment because she was interned, and so forth. But that wasn't true. If she had pains or symptoms, she could go for tests. But without them – as you might say for no reason, just because she was worried, or for prevention – no, she couldn't.'

'I don't understand. I don't believe that you went for the scan like that, for no reason.'

To his astonishment, she replied, 'Yes, I did, more or less.'

He tried to smile, but it was sour.

'So as I understand it, you both went to the doctor for no reason. First you, then Linda.'

The girl took a deep breath.

'Calm down. These things are hard to explain. It wasn't just a whim, as it might seem. Especially not in Linda's case. I'll try to be clear, but please, don't get irritated.' The girl caressed his neck. 'All right?'

In a gentle voice she began explaining the regulations governing the medical care of high-level officials and their families. There was a programme of preventive medicine for senior cadres. He had heard vaguely of such a thing for Politburo members and perhaps for ministers too. But the scheme had been extended even into the provinces. Migena's father, although without an official position, had benefitted, and consequently Migena had too, and so the story of the breast scan began. A doctor had arrived from Tirana and Migena went for the scan, accompanied by Linda. On the way . . .

As she talked, he imagined how, on the way, her friend had come out with the idea of being examined herself, and how death had chosen that moment to take revenge for being treated so lightly. A revenge as cruel as only death knew, and if not on both of them, then on Linda.

'On the way,' Migena continued, 'Linda asked me to help her . . .'

He barely interrupted her, and at the end of the story she seemed so drained that when she asked 'May I sleep a little?' her words seemed to him the most natural in the world.

He kissed her temples and took care that her shoulders were covered. He had never heard such an unhappy story in his life and perhaps never would again.

Her soft breathing gave a different rhythm to the events as they sank into his memory. With Migena asleep, at one remove from life, he thought about her story of what had happened in that small provincial town, in the little hospital where a doctor had inconspicuously arrived from the capital city.

The girls had made fragmentary conversation as they walked together along the deserted road towards the hospital. 'Are you worried?' Linda asked, and Migena replied, 'I don't know what to say, but I'm uneasy. In these cases, even when the examination is . . . for no reason . . . you worry.' To her surprise, Linda seemed more unnerved than she was. 'Listen,' she said in a faint voice. 'You've done so much for me, I'll be grateful to you for ever, and I don't want to take advantage in any way, but I would ask you for one more thing. I don't have the slightest chance of having a scan. I don't know if you can help me . . .'

Migena smiled. 'Darling, I'll do anything for you, with all my heart, but why do you need it? You've told me that you have no symptoms, not even the slightest suspicion.'

'I do have a reason,' Linda replied. 'A different reason, a very serious one.'

So there *is* a reason, Migena thought. A terrible and irreversible one, which she had kept secret. Not to have any regrets perhaps. As if internment were not enough for this girl, now there was this.

Linda received Migena's emotional embrace with a certain coldness. 'It's not what you think. I told you, I haven't any suspicions, there are no signs.'

'What?' Migena cried almost angrily. 'Are you playing games with me?'

Linda tried to explain. It wasn't a game, not at all. The truth was that she had no pain, no suspicions, but still she was ready to do almost anything for that scan. It was her only chance, her only hope.

Her only chance, Migena repeated to herself. Chance of what?

What she heard next was worse than cruel. The explanation turned Migena's brain inside out until finally she understood. This scan was the only chance for Linda to go to the longed-for capital city – if the result was unfavourable. A cousin, interned like herself, had told her that these were the only tests to which internees were entitled, and they were carried out at the Oncological Hospital in Tirana. Patients could travel by train to an appointment once a month. For practical reasons, they had to spend the night at a hotel and return the next day by train. The treatment would last from six to eight months. 'Do you understand now why this is the last chance? Call me crazy, but in my situation it's the only chance. Many women would do this.'

Here Migena paused in her story. 'I conceded she was right. I would have done the same. In Linda's place, I would also have traded endless years of internment for six months of life, and perhaps, like a gift from heaven, the danger would have passed.'

When the hospital came into view, Linda's eyes sparkled with gratitude. There was now only the anxiety over whether the doctor would accept her.

'Fortunately he was young and had been trained abroad. I did all I could. I told him she was my closest friend, and was concerned, but her family were not officials. He was hesitant but I think her beauty won him over. We both went into the anteroom to remove our blouses. It was the first time that we had seen each other's breasts. I have a reason for mentioning this matter of our breasts. Please don't interrupt.'

Dazed but happy they emerged from the dark X-ray room. Their cheeks glowed, and as they left the building Linda continually whispered to Migena. She had worked it all out in detail. Ever since Migena told her to come to the hospital, Linda had been working out a plan which even she thought was crazy at first, but could not dispel from her mind. She pictured the features of the city that she had dreamed of for so long, and would finally see for herself. She brought to mind all the things they had talked about, one by one. She would meet Rudian Stefa. She knew that she was beautiful and she didn't like to pretend otherwise. She would phone him and tell him straight out: I'm the girl to whom you sent a book inscribed to Linda B. I'd like us to get to know each other.

The need for a hotel was a miracle, she kept saying. None of her family could accompany her because they were all interned.

'Every one of them interned . . .' Migena spoke these last words like the refrain of that old song of the Albanians from Calabria, 'All Beneath the Earth'.

'Do you remember it?' asked Migena, and she sang:

> *There is my strong father*
> *There is my gentle mother*
> *There is my brother*
> *All beneath the earth.*

As the date for the results drew closer, Linda's imagination ran riot. Her idea now – after saying, I'd like us to get to know each other – was to give Rudian the name of her hotel and the room number. She was serious about meeting him, as in everything she did, and was conscious that they had no time to waste. She had to be prepared for everything, and remembered the irritating fact of her virginity. She even thought of her gym teacher, whom she alone of the girls from her class had hitherto treated with indifference.

Rudian had thought that Migena might stop her story at any moment. He barely kept himself from asking: And then . . . ? His mind raced ahead like a bolting animal. Of course this story ended badly. But what happened next?

It was not long now until the decisive day. As if scared, the two girls avoided talking about it. But their silence could not banish the dark shadow, and only intensified its presence. As Rudian listened to Migena, he thought of how death, having been trifled with, might take its revenge. An aggressive tumour, found too late. Another reason for suicide might be an unexpected change to the Regulations of Internment: Paragraph 12, Subsection 4, Withdrawal of right to travel to Tirana for breast cancer treatment.

The results arrived at the end of the week. The assistant doctor congratulated both girls, but was astonished at their reaction. First they stood dumbfounded, then embraced each another, but coldly, as if in a chill lunar light. The tears contained more sorrow than they should have done.

'I don't know how to describe it. Everything was turned inside out, joy turning to grief and back again.' Vaguely, Migena offered a strange, inapt consolation.

Two reasons for suicide were now eliminated, Rudian thought. The only one left was for Linda to have killed herself because no cancer had appeared.

No. There was a limit to perversity. This was too much under any regime, however cruel.

Rudian's mind slowed down to take in this new information. Here, at the end of the twentieth century, was a young girl who'd thought of an unfavourable breast scan as her last chance, almost her salvation. A good result was bad news, an end to all her hopes. Even at the price of death, she'd wanted to buy a few days, a few hours of normal life. But her offer had been rejected.

Rudian tried to imagine himself in Linda's place. All her dreams had collapsed. Migena was going away. The prospect of endless loneliness. No wonder she thought of cancer as her salvation. People had become used to thinking of death like this, but not yet cancer.

He had no right to . . . he said to himself vaguely. Then he lost the thread. What didn't he have a right to? He had no right, in any event. That was it – he had no right to be surprised.

The stronger the dictatorship of the proletariat, the greater the freedom! This slogan was displayed everywhere, on the walls of auditoriums, on balconies, beneath the state emblem. Everybody walked past these fluttering red banners without the slightest consternation. Why then should people rub their eyes to read a similar text, almost its twin: *Cancer brings happiness!*

Migena was exhausted from talking, and she told him she wanted to sleep a little.

He stroked her hair and said quietly, 'It was what I suspected. The result of the scan upset her.' Yet it had not been a bad result, but a good one: I don't have cancer, I don't want to live anymore.

How dreadful, he thought.

Migena's eyes widened, and she shook her head in denial.

'We'll talk some more, darling,' she whispered. 'Let me rest now.'

He wanted to tell her to wait, but the girl's altered breathing told him it was too late.

So it wasn't the scan. He wanted to wake her and howl: If not this scan, what the hell was it? Why this silence when you should speak? What happened? Did you come between us? That's the reason. The enigma? I thought I was the reason, with that damned book and its inscription. Then the breast scan, I believed that. Now it turns out to be something else. So who was it? There's no one left but you. Why did you do it? Or rather, why did you tell her?'

More than anything else, it was the girl's quiet breathing that led him to suspect that Migena was hiding the answer. She had mentioned in passing an evening dance, and the recollection of this thrummed insistently through his mind. He had interrupted her two or three times to ask about that evening, but the girl had responded curtly, as if it were unimportant. It was the school graduation ball, the farewell dance . . . Didn't they have them in his day?

He could hardly wait to ask her properly, which it struck him he had not done before.

Her breathing suggested that she was waking up at last. Amazingly, all the imagined brusqueness of his question melted away and he whispered tenderly into her ear, 'So, it wasn't the scan. It was a different reason, wasn't it? Try to tell me what happened. Did you put yourself between us?'

'I was expecting this question,' she said.

He imagined, rather than saw, her wintry smile. And also the ironic glitter in her eyes, mixed with anger.

'I don't blame you for asking,' she said. 'I would have thought the same.'

'I didn't mean any harm,' Rudian said. 'Any person in my position would just want to know the truth. I've thought so often that it was all my fault. Inadvertently, of course, but that's no reassurance—'

'I'm not blaming you,' the girl interrupted. 'Don't you know what torture it's been for me? I've suffered. I've cried so much, you know I have. Whenever you've shouted at me and hit me.'

'I've never hit you.'

'You've meant to, which is the same thing. You've yelled at me, called me a spy, screamed, What's the matter with you? Now I think you understand what the matter was.'

'I'm sorry, I meant no harm.'

For a while nothing could be heard but their breathing, the two currents of air intertwined, as tangled as they were themselves.

'I took everything from her,' the girl said softly. 'They had seized her family's house, their property and jewels. I took from her the last thing she had, what she held most precious, the only thing . . .' He wanted to stop her mouth and not to hear it, but the word came out: 'You.'

He wanted to tell her she had been kind. It had caused her tears and she had searched her conscience. But words seemed to him feeble and unnecessary.

'We're still not being honest,' the girl said. 'We don't dare, either of us. We evade the truth, the dangerous part. We're scared.'

'I'm not,' he said.

'Naturally, it's all down to me. But you know something too. You can't avoid it. You know that I was starting to fall in love with you.'

Of course he knew, but it was outside the order of things. Once again Rudian could no longer think clearly, and Migena's words, as if under his influence, became more obscure. Obviously, Migena's love wasn't her own. It belonged to her interned friend. She had found it ready-made. It was like wild clematis on someone else's wall. A ring found somewhere. Is love contagious, like a disease? Apparently it was. She had caught it from Linda B. on her journeys between her friend and him. As if upon entering a contaminated area, Migena had been infected. She had gone to and fro happily without it occurring to her what might happen . . . Well, it was easy to assume that she hadn't thought of it, but maybe the opposite was true: not only had she thought of it, but something had impelled her unconsciously towards him. There was a dark, perverse logic in it all. It was easy to say that she had taken her girlfriend's lover. That's a very popular sport. But there was something else. Her friend too, in her powerlessness, with the same perversity with which she had wished cancer on herself, had pushed Migena in his direction, within his grasp.

Jealousy? Their story had all the ingredients of a romance, but with one difference. The events were always hidden behind a veil drawn by an unknown power, and seemed to come from the realm of destiny. It was this that upset the everyday equilibrium, logic and the order of things. Migena had been jealous of Linda, but very obliquely, under a mask of the opposite. Linda B. had also felt jealous of Migena, but still more covertly and beneath a double mask.

Their mutual resentment had risen close to the surface, but stopped there. On one occasion, when Migena thought Linda was about to grab her by the hair, just as he had once done by the bookshelves, she thought: Of course, I'm her understudy – the other two are the protagonists in this affair. In fact, this was the most accurate word: 'understudy'.

Rudian's temples beat feverishly. What did 'understudy' mean in this context? Everything was so obscure.

He wanted to say that she was less an understudy than a courier of some kind, striving to do the impossible, to bring from a forbidden zone something that could not be transported – a girl's love. It was not just impossible, but a crime against nature.

Something occurred to him that was still more difficult to put into words. A courier of death, he said to himself. But there was no way you could carry death.

Coming close to what he was thinking, the girl said, 'It's no use trying to excuse ourselves.'

Her eyes glinted dangerously, as if to say: We both killed her.

Perhaps, he thought. However invisibly, he too had played just as sinister a role in this.

'There's no need to punish yourself,' he said in a gentle voice. 'You've suffered in your conscience. That's enough. In this country, nobody has a bad conscience about anything.'

He caressed her and kissed the curls at her temples.

We didn't kill her, he thought. We just failed to get her out of that place. And that's not the same thing.

Migena made no sign of objection. With a distracted expression, she watched sidelong as he stroked her chest, but now absent-mindedly, as if he were a stranger.

The girl still followed the movement of his hand. Then, to his astonishment, she murmured something very unclear, as if trying to say that there, in her breasts, there was something.

So death is there. The thought of the scan flashed through Rudian's mind, and he mentioned it again. But she shook her head in denial.

That only left jealousy. They were back in the whirl-pool of often-repeated themes. Cerberus not being lulled to sleep. The secret jealousy of one of the girls. Then the other's jealousy, even more deeply hidden. Love passed on like a disease. Could it be given and received like a jewel, a loan or a legacy? The goddess Aphrodite had lent it to her female friends in the form of a girdle, tied round the hips, close to where the thighs meet. In a tangible form. As for conveying love from place to place, this was apparently more difficult, perhaps even more dangerous than the fearful transportation of plutonium. There could be no doubt that jealousy was all that was left.

I'm not asking you why you came to me. I'm asking something else. How did she find out? Why did you tell her?

'I didn't want to,' the girl replied. 'It happened un-expectedly, at the ball.'

Don't! he wailed to himself. Again, it had turned out he was to blame.

'Why did I tell her? I don't know. It seemed to me that she knew. But wait, that wasn't the reason. Calm down. I swear to you by everything I hold dear, it wasn't what you think. Jealousy wasn't the problem. Not at all. It was some-thing else, entirely different, there at the ball . . .'

12

T HE MORE indistinct her speech became, as if she were under an anaesthetic, the more clearly he imagined the farewell ball.

It was twenty years since Rudian had experienced one of those evenings, but he remembered exactly what they were like – merciless.

Breathless snatches of tango merged into one another under the languid gaze of the dancers. Dances for couples were interspersed with folk dances, in which the students held hands and spread a wide circle to include hesitant wallflowers, then their teachers and the school director. The principal guest – the district's Party secretary – looked on.

Slow music started again, with dewy-eyed boys getting drunk for the first time, sighing girls, ambiguous remarks on both sides, and pangs, endless pangs over words left unsaid.

The school's guests watched the hubbub in the room from among the beer bottles at the top table. As their fears of possible lapses of behaviour receded, their tender feelings towards the pupils, their own children among them, warmed the atmosphere. The young people deserved a party after finishing school, and their volunteer work projects too, and despite the malicious gossip their moral fibre was strong. Look, even tonight, the most unbuttoned evening of all, they had remembered to include folk dances, partisan songs, and especially the newly minted song 'Leader, Our Leader, Long Life to You'.

The clamour sometimes yielded to the strains of the tango, sometimes it stubbornly persisted. Besides couples of boys and girls, there were occasional pairings of girls, and more rarely boys. As usual, there were plenty of boys dancing with the literature teacher, and pairs of teachers together. There was the director and his wife, waiting for the success of the evening to be crowned when the principal guest stood up to join the dancing. But this usually happened just before the end. Midnight was still far away and for the moment the atmosphere was of general nostalgia, whispered tête-à-têtes, entrances and exits for no reason, and endless trips to the toilet.

From the top table, Migena's father looked for his daughter among the throng. In spite of her pleading, he was wearing all his decorations, having assured her that it would be for the last time. It was not boasting, he had said that afternoon. For years on end he had worked silently for the state, and he had promised her that he would wear all these medals only twice in her presence: at her graduation ball and, fate permitting, at her wedding. Now he was following her with his eyes, as if to say:

I don't think I'll make it to your wedding, so forgive me for this evening.

In the midst of the crowd, Migena and Linda were dancing together again. They were in great demand from the boys, but this was the second time they had managed to shake them off.

'You're going away. You'll leave me alone,' Linda said.

Migena trembled. Don't, she wanted to say. Just don't talk like that.

She felt she understood why Linda's latest hairstyle had not just impressed but also frightened her. A vague unease suggested to her that this style was perfectly suited to Linda's words. Migena was going to leave her alone. The gleaming grip in Linda's hair seemed to hold in its clasp all the things they were attempting to hide.

Migena missed her chance. She didn't know what to say. It was the last opportunity for words left unsaid, perhaps their moment of farewell. Would they manage a third dance together?

She caught the gaze of the gym teacher. His look seemed to offer her a kind of rescue, a postponement of the fatal conversation. Why was he staring at Linda like that? 'You've stuck in his memory, no doubt,' Migena said. 'Perhaps,' Linda replied indifferently. She was about to say something, but she hesitated. 'Perhaps it's not his fault. I think, when I had hopes of going to Tirana, I may have given him a sign. You can imagine why.' 'I understand,' Migena said.

The teacher looked at Linda, his bewildered eyes asking why she was pretending not to know him.

To Migena, a tango had never seemed so long. She smelled Linda's fragrance – an unfamiliar, light perfume, perhaps from the days of the monarchy. Most of the time they did not speak, until Linda uttered those words that Migena feared most of all: 'How can you leave me?'

'I didn't know what to say. All words were meaningless. I couldn't say that I was not going to leave her, or anything like that. I knew more than anyone that there could be no consolation. It was obvious how she would end up, a primary school teacher on some remote collective farm, if not worse – milking cows in the co-operative, working in the cattle sheds or in the scrubby pastures beside the fields, where she would have to give herself to the brigade-leader, or he would make her life hell.

'You were my last hope, she said to me. I wanted to clap my hand over her mouth and tell her to stop but I couldn't even do that. Bring me news from the outside world . . . from him . . .

'The more she talked, the more at fault I felt. How could I leave her, with my conscience still burdened by this guilt? That evening was the last chance. I had mentally rehearsed the difficult explanation, involving you, so many times. I thought of the pain I would cause. That was the worst of all. I would have preferred her anger – if she had said, Cheat! You took from me my only joy!

then I could have said, Don't talk to me like that. It's your own fault.

'I thought I had a certain justification. As I said, I was convinced that Linda had pushed me towards you. Her eyes shone whenever your name was in the newspaper and especially when you appeared on television. She repeated things you said. Sometimes she would ask me, Do you fancy him? Tell me, don't you fancy him a little? And she would immediately cap this by saying that any girl who goes with him is lucky.'

And so the evening wore on. Migena was no longer sure if she wanted it to finish, or to continue endlessly until the moment . . . Her hesitation had tortured her for so long, but as much as she wanted to shed its burden, she could not bear to hurt Linda. It might be the final straw.

Midnight was approaching, the hour that somehow seemed the most dangerous of all. They were now dancing apart, with boys, but they caught each other's eyes above the dancers' shoulders as they whirled ever faster. They could hardly wait to be together again, and suddenly once more they were.

The band played louder. The Party secretary had left with some of the important guests and as usual the saxophonist, restrained until then, seized the chance to let rip.

The musician, pleased at the attention he was getting, shook his loose locks and smiled at Linda.

She returned his smile absent-mindedly, as if from the moon. She put her lips to Migena's ear and whispered, 'At least, if you had got close to him.' Migena could not tell if she had really heard these words or only imagined them, as if in a dream, because perhaps she had been expecting them. Linda moved her face away to look her in the eye, and added, 'Did you hear what I said? At least, if you had gone with him.'

Migena trembled. They were the same words, but with a difference: instead of saying 'got close to him' she had now used a different, more ruthless and almost vulgar phrase, 'if you had gone with him.'

A protracted shriek came from the saxophone. Migena froze. Perhaps it was her only form of self-defence: to remain immobile, not giving or taking anything. Linda's words were indistinct. Migena could avoid them, but not her look. The realisation that Linda had understood what had happened struck her like a body blow. She couldn't tell what expression her face revealed. She still wasn't sure if she had really heard those words or not.

Disconnected words tumbled from Linda's lips, or did it simply suit Migena to interpret them that way? Were they frightening words under the mask of ordinariness, or the other way round? It's not a question of guilt . . . don't people say, Give him a kiss from me . . . forgiveness, in church . . . for no reason . . . betrayal . . . you were the only one, darling, do I have to tell you a hundred times? . . . if you really got it together . . . faithful friend.

Although her words were vague, her look was clear, questioning, urgent. Migena didn't say anything, but embraced her fiercely, and that was enough. There was no need for tears or words. Linda understood.

Migena waited for what would happen next. Linda's face turned even whiter. But her eyes retained something of their earlier look. That was the only hope.

Suddenly, Linda responded to her embrace, and Migena was flooded with a heavenly peace. Years ago, in a dream, she had once experienced something similar, in a sort of garden with creatures like deer. But it had been very brief. Just let it last a bit longer, she prayed. Just a little. Oh God.

As if her prayer had been heard, the peace continued. Linda's voice was not only reassuring, but was uttering familiar-sounding words. They were the same words from before, which Migena had thought were garbled. Now she was surprised to understand their meaning. 'There's no reason for you to feel guilty, it's something that happens. It isn't betrayal, you've been my most faithful friend for so many years. You've done so much for me, and even this time it was something like friendship that led you on, I'm sure. Don't people say, Give him a hug, or a kiss from me? We're not in church here, asking forgiveness. Can you hear me, darling?'

Migena wanted to close her eyes as she listened to the murmuring voice. The sounds of the tango were more appropriate than ever. Some people nearby were watching them curiously. Migena felt a twinge of anxiety, but forgot them.

'And please don't ask me again to forgive you. I'm being honest. I'm not saying I'm happy about it, but believe me, I almost knew it would happen. Because – let me confess to something I thought I'd take with me to the grave. Let me admit it. Secretly, I wanted it to happen, I won't hide it. I felt jealous when I imagined it. But it's hard for me to fully explain. Secretly, I wanted it. It was the only chance for something, a part of me, to make the leap . . .'

'I wanted to tell her that I had vaguely felt the same. And not just that. I wanted to tell her that you too, Rudian, felt something unusual. You were a person sensitive to ghosts. I wanted to tell her about the scenes when you were angry, and shouting, Why the hell are you crying? and when you were hitting me, and even suspecting I was a spy . . . I did not tell her any of these things, except the last bit, when you shouted: Only if you are a spy.'

Linda tried to smile, and raised the palm of her hand to her mouth as if to say: No, stop, there will be time for you to tell me everything.

Her sudden animation frightened Migena. What did she mean by those words? Time to talk was precisely what they would no longer have, but Migena did not remind her of this. If Linda were even remotely upset by her confession, she was ready to give up Rudian. After all, Migena was only an accessory, an interlude. A kind of understudy. He is yours. Your prince. Nothing in the world can separate you.

An unsteady gleam flickered in Linda's eyes, which became now dull, now crystal clear. 'Listen,' she said. Migena should get rid of the idea that she felt defeated. On the contrary, she felt easier. A part of her dream had come true. Thanks to Migena, she no longer felt so confined. As she had said before, a part of her had made the leap and would never come back. Moreover, Migena would bring news from him, messages . . .

Linda was indeed smiling, but with the smile of someone who is in two minds whether to speak again. 'Listen,' she said again at last. 'Don't think that I'm perfect myself. Do you remember when you told me about Mr Right-Off?' – their private nickname for the gym teacher – 'You were in an emotional state, like all girls after they lose their virginity, and then you felt remorse, that perhaps he hadn't been the right person, and I told you not to worry, that's how most girls start off, with write-offs. So, you were honest with me, but I wasn't honest with you. No need to stare at me like that.'

She told Migena how at the time of what they had come to call the famous breast scan, one afternoon in the gym changing room before a volleyball match, she had given a clear sign to Mr Right-Off.

At any other time Migena would naturally have asked: And then? But on that evening she realised that she didn't want to hear. They had both been dishonest with each other. That was some consolation. But now the symmetry was broken, and only Migena would be left with her dishonesty, as before.

But Linda did not continue the story. Either there was no sequel, and her sign had remained just a sign, or she had sensed that Migena did not want to know.

They both smiled, futile fugitive smiles, until Linda's eyes again hardened into crystal. She said something about fate, which Migena, abstracted, didn't catch. It was something about the hand of fate drawing them both to the same men, whether on the lower plane of Mr Right-Off or the higher plane of the playwright.

'Strange, isn't it? Linda said. Then she reached out and shook me as if to make sure I had really grasped how extraordinary it was that we were both steered by a higher power.

'Another protracted wail came from the saxophone. Soon the ball would start winding down. The school director and the secretary of the youth organisation were looking very worried at the direction the evening had taken.

'We danced for a while in silence. I wondered if I might have misinterpreted the understanding she had shown for me. Was her outward calm in fact false? In my attempts at consolation, was I behaving like a drowning woman clutching at her own hair?'

When Linda finally opened her mouth to speak, her expression had totally changed. Migena trembled as she began talking quietly about something that she had never mentioned: her internment. Three months ago, one week before Migena had brought her Rudian Stefa's book, her family had received their 'directive'. Linda explained that this was what they called the order that came every five years, on the precise day on which they had completed five years' internment. It was always brief and unequivocal, and there were two possibilities: your internment was either terminated or extended for another five-year term.

A five-year term, Migena repeated to herself, trying to get used to the idea. It sounded like the five-year plan, but something grim and tight-lipped, like a death mask, whereas the five-year plan meant festivities and jubilation.

Linda had returned from school that day to find an unaccustomed silence at home. Her parents were sitting by the window. There were traces of tears in her mother's eyes. She understood immediately. They had been waiting for days. But still she asked, 'Did it come?' Her mother nodded. She didn't need to ask anything else.

She embraced her parents without a word. Her little brother had still not returned from his ball game. Five years before, when she was thirteen, it had been more or less the same. But it had hurt less, or so it seemed to her. Linda's brother, only five years old, had understood nothing. This was the first time that they would have to tell him. Then five more endless years would pass. They would gather together every Christmas and New Year's Eve, exchange wishes for a 'Happy New Year' and add, 'and good luck with the directive.' Oh God!

Migena wanted to ask her, please, to stop, but she couldn't. Two or three times Linda's little brother had asked, 'What's a directive?' They told him it was news that came in an envelope and nobody knew if it would be good or bad. Only when you opened the envelope. And when he insisted on asking where it came from, they said from Tirana, reminding him not to tell anyone, because the directive was secret and talking about it might spoil its magic power.

The dancing continued. Migena had never imagined that the sounds of music could do so much to amplify sorrow as well as joy. All around them was loud laughter, banter, an excited heaving throng. Quietly, Linda described what had gone through her mind on that bitter day. She was eighteen, and the next directive would arrive when she was twenty-three. Then twenty-eight. Two more directives and then thirty-eight, and then finally forty-three. She had no desire to live beyond that. Thank you, dictatorship of the proletariat, I know that you are a good thing, just and infallible, as we learned at school, but I'm tired . . . I've had enough of this life.

The laughter continued around them. The mingling of boys' and girls' voices was particularly hard to bear.

'Do you understand? I've never lived a single day in freedom,' Linda said. 'Can you imagine what that's like? Not one day. With no hopes of anybody . . . because I never knew where to look for hope. So cancer was my last chance. I asked for its help, but it didn't help me either.'

Migena could hardly contain a sob. She wanted to offer to take her place, at least for one five-year term, but she was unable to utter a word.

The sound of the saxophone ripped through everything like a knife.

Migena, instead of offering to take her place in internment, began, without knowing why – perhaps out of sympathy – to tell Linda something she had sworn never to reveal. She had made this promise to her father, and in fact it was his secret, a terrible thing he had read in a confidential bulletin that was distributed only to trusted Party officials, but which for some reason he had told his daughter. The bulletin printed what enemies of the state had said. Among other things, they claimed that there was no freedom, not only in prisons and in internment, but even outside. In other words there was no freedom anywhere, not even in Tirana. That is what our enemies are saying, of course.

Linda said nothing for a while. Then she repeated Migena's phrase: Of course. Of course. It depended on your viewpoint – to a prisoner shackled in his cell, an internee like Linda might seem free. In which case she had no reason to complain. Linda might say the same of Rudian, who was complaining about the treatment of his play, and so on. It was all very complicated, like the universe itself, which they'd talked about so much, infinite time and space, totally beyond their conception.

Linda returned to the unforgettable week after the arrival of the directive. 'We were all dumbfounded. You were in Tirana, and I could hardly wait for you to come back. I had never missed you so much. And then, as if you knew, you returned with that miracle in your hand, his book.'

To say that his book restored her to life would be the least of it. She opened it dozens, hundreds of times to read its dedication, *For Linda B., a souvenir from the author.*

Migena was well aware of the effect of this gift. Linda had been a fan of the playwright and almost in love with him, but it was the book that had turned her head completely. Everything else paled in comparison – her internment and the fatal directive. She thought only of him, to the point that she felt ashamed. 'When you told me that he had problems at the theatre and his play might be banned, I broke down completely. I dreamed of being close to him, laying my head on his shoulder, consoling him, saying, Darling, don't worry, it will pass.'

Migena barely contained her tears. Perhaps she, the understudy, should have consoled Rudian in this way. But there was no hint of reproach in Linda's words. It was as if everything they had just said had been wiped out.

The band abruptly fell silent and the dancers turned their heads to see what was happening. Angry voices could be heard, probably an ordinary quarrel among boys, inevitable at these evenings and now well overdue. The band struck up once more and the separated dancers came together again. Others had migrated to the toilets. Migena and Linda unthinkingly headed in that direction. Curious eyes followed them. The toilet doors swung open and shut incessantly. Boys were smoking cigarettes half in secret. Passages shrouded in semi-darkness led off the main corridor. Migena and Linda wandered blindly towards them, perhaps to get away from the noise of the doors and the unpleasant odour. The sound of the band receded. Here and there, the silhouettes of couples could be seen. Linda pushed open a door, surprised that the chemistry laboratory should have been left open. They entered and stood between the open door and the long shelves of bottles and test tubes. A pale light illuminated the inscriptions on the bottles, which they knew so well: potassium bicarbonate; the two rival acids – sulphuric and hydrochloric – which stuck in their memories from their many exams and also the vindictive rage of a classmate who out of jealousy had vowed to disfigure the face of a girl in 3B with H_2SO_4. Next came the poisons, their cold bottles no doubt locked up, as if sequestered from this world. 'What a lot of poisons,' Linda said quietly.

The music could barely be heard except for the saxophone, whose piercing shriek grew louder. The silence lasted longer than it should have done and Migena silently prayed that Linda would not resume the conversation about internment, but it seemed to her that it was Linda's right to speak first.

Linda was attentively studying her friend's face. With a gentle, dream-like movement her fingers touched Migena's lower lip, and then both lips together.

'How strange,' she said. 'These lips have been kissed. By his lips.'

'I didn't know how to reply. It was too awful for words. I couldn't cope with it.

'How strange, she said again, and drew her lips to mine. It was an odd kiss, stiff and frigid. In this way we kissed each other, until Linda asked, Did you go further?

'Any delay in my reply would have been fatal. So would telling the truth. These thoughts did not come to me clearly, yet I felt both of them like an electrical discharge. I had to reply at once, and at all costs conceal the truth.

'I shook my head in denial, without taking my eyes off her, convinced that this was the only way.

'No, I said aloud, he only stroked my breasts.

'What more could I say? She didn't ask anything else. With her delicate fingers she unfastened the buttons of her blouse while her other hand searched for my own. She wore no bra, and neither did I, which was the recent fashion among girls who felt confident in their figures. She drew my hand to her breasts, whispered, Do it like him, and stood motionless with her eyes half-closed. An icy shiver ran through us as if a door into the unknown had suddenly been opened.

'We were not lesbians, either of us. It was something else.'

Rudian imagined this moment, and he thought of it during the hours and days that followed, without being able to define what it was. It was something stranger than lesbianism, more singular, and doubtless more transgressive. There was no name for it. Nothing that had happened between the girls had a name yet, especially the experience of that moment. They were both close and distant. Two girls inter-, supra-, trans-caressing. And between them: frozen, uncomprehending, soulless spaces. If Migena was a courier of death, as he had said, what role was left for Linda? A girl who sent her body a long distance to perform the rites of love, without which she would find no peace? Usually it was the opposite, the soul rushing to overcome obstacles, while the body remained a physical hostage to a place. But here something unprecedented was happening. Her body was striving to acquire the characteristics of a soul, or if it were not her own body, then its simulacrum, or understudy . . . the body of her closest friend.

They were both beyond the laws of this world. In consequence, what had happened must have been unprecedented in the history of the planet. Something appointed by destiny, to be accomplished by two girls – daughters of socialism, as the phrase went – in a godforsaken Albanian province at the end of the twentieth century.

During this part of the story, Rudian Stefa had felt for the second time, yet more hopelessly, a slab-like weight on his chest. You bastard, he thought. You rat. Nothing he had written would have any value after this.

Linda held her breath. Only in this way could she catch the quiet scraping noise, accompanied by what seemed like faint, very faint voices, which she had dimly sensed before Migena mentioned them to her.

It was real. Something like the scraping of a door, some very soft voices, and a muffled scream or perhaps a burst of laughter froze her completely.

In panic, Linda covered her chest, and craned her head to the right and left. Migena whispered, 'Perhaps it's our imagination.' But nothing could still their shaking terror.

They went out into the corridor and in confusion walked in the direction of the music. There was not a soul to be seen, and Migena said again that perhaps they were imagining things.

The familiar din of the ball drew closer. They passed the toilet doors, still slamming. Boys with cigarettes, a few holding beer bottles and with dangerous looks. At last, the safety of the hubbub that seemed now to have reached its peak.

They plunged into the sea of dancers, and hoped not to look conspicuous as they followed each other, looking for a safe corner. They pretended nothing had happened, but were scared by the glances of alarm that focused on them. Some curious onlookers put their heads together to whisper, and then broke into laughter. The teacher on duty wore a glacial expression. Somebody mentioned the poet Sappho and then something about modern ways. It was useless to pretend they didn't understand.

What had happened? Who had seen them? How had the rumour spread so fast? Nothing could be understood in the noisy confusion now drowning every word. Between the savagery of the band and the wail of the saxophone that grew louder with every dance, furtive whispering counted for nothing.

How was she able to rise above it all? Where did she find the strength?

Migena would ask herself these questions many times later, but at that moment she could think only of how to escape. Linda, who so rarely lost her cool head, seemed even worse. She was the first to say 'Let's go'. But also the first to hesitate: 'No, better stay.'

Any last hope that their panic might have been excessive was dashed when they heard Flora Dulaku of 4B pipe up, 'You were hiding away?' Her squire erupted into laughter. 'Leave them be, it takes all sorts.' Somebody to their right butted in with: 'New experiences.'

'Scum,' Migena burst out, unable to hold back her tears.

To their horror, the ball was ending. The saxophonist gave a farewell howl until he looked about to collapse on the floor, and everything stopped.

Among the shouts, farewell embraces and tears, they were now the only ones excluded. Like does cornered by hunters they ran to the exit, not knowing that worse things awaited them there.

A boy puffed his cigarette smoke in the couple's hair, and followed it with a savage whistle, while another trailed beside them, wailing 'Decadence,' then 'Life on Lesbos,' and a little further on the phrase 'the whole world' came up again, this time drawn out in the song:

Lovely breasts like yours,
The whole world will adore.

Another boy shouted to his mate, 'Hey Blendi, Blendi,' and completed the verse:

Lucky the girl who's tried them.
She'll live for evermore.

More shouts came: Hey Blendi, classic, eh? Get the difference? Lucky the *girl* who's tried them. *Girl*, not *boy*. Ha ha, phew! Bunch of lezzies.

The whistling grew wilder. How had their assailants managed to take up positions so far away, like in an ambush? The darkness thickened and the whistling came out of the murk, blind and cruel. 'Over here, Linda.' 'No, go away.' 'I'll walk you home.' 'No, I'll go myself. Go away. No . . .'

'And so we parted, without coming to any understanding. I didn't know if I would see her again.'

Even before she finished, Rudian knew what had happened the next day in the little provincial town. On that confused, damp morning when Migena left early on the long-distance bus, the meetings would have already begun. At the Party Committee, for sure. At the Secretariat for Internal Affairs. In the school. The neighbourhood. *Class enemies, although facing defeat, are still active. After their sabotage and conspiracies have failed, these hostile forces have resorted to different tactics, using perversion and sex.*

For two days Linda did not leave her home. She could endure no more. It was not hard to find poison in this agricultural town.

Her parents discovered her in the morning, totally discoloured. A sheet of paper on which she had apparently wanted to write something remained blank.

They buried her that same afternoon, using the municipal cart that did service whenever the hearse broke down. A lock of chestnut hair poked out from the blanket covering her body on the open bier, which swayed with the movement of the cart. Her parents and little brother followed with a municipal employee and, a few paces behind them, a stranger with a cap and the collar of his overcoat raised.

This stranger in the dark coat who didn't want to be recognised provided a last curious twist to the story. Most people suspected him to be someone to do with Internal Affairs. But others said with lowered voices that this secret mourner was none other than the gym teacher.

13

TWO WEEKS LATER. RUDIAN STEFA'S MORNING

H<small>E WOKE</small> at more or less the time he thought it was, about eleven. This was a good sign. He didn't like to find it was twelve, when he expected it to be half past five, or the other way round. But still he swore under his breath, spluttering and letting rip with mankind's most common expletive that serves for any occasion. Dreaming of it brings good luck, they say.

He emerged from the bathroom with a few protracted yawns and among them, unrelated to any flu or cold, a strong, emptily triumphant sneeze that rang through the apartment.

His legs carried him against his will to his desk, where his papers had lain scattered in disorder since yesterday. He bent over them with almost childish curiosity, as if he believed they might have written themselves during the night.

What he saw was not encouraging. The mercilessly crossed-out lines loomed black, and the survivors huddled awkwardly, as if cowering in shame amidst the carnage. He let out a deep breath and his mood plummeted. What a hell of a business, he thought, swallowing with difficulty that other word he had recently tried hard to avoid in his writing.

He started to read.

Act One. Scene One. Warehouse at the copper-enrichment plant. Sacks or trucks full of ore. Brigade-leader SHPEND *and his* ASSISTANT *at work on them. Enter* HUNGARIAN ADVISER.

HUNGARIAN ADVISER (*greeting them*): Good morning, comrades!

SHPEND *and his* ASSISTANT (*in chorus*): Good morning, Comrade Imre!

ADVISER: Vairy neece weather, yes?

SHPEND *and* ADVISER: Lovely.

The word was unavoidable as Rudian crunched the paper into a ball. He wanted to weep.

The week before, on the psychiatrist's advice and in an attempt to avert depression, he had decided to start a new play. He had found an old synopsis in his notes, which looked surprisingly promising; in an industrial plant producing copper for export, traces of gold are unexpectedly found in the ore.

Like most of his notes, the synopsis was both concise and very vague. The phrases bore little relation to one another. After *Gold in the copper ore?* came the word 'strange' – twice even. Then identical trucks: black, boring, carrying who knew what substance. Then incomprehensible phrases, as if they had something to hide. Which country was the customer? In fact there were two. The first country, the earlier customer, belonged to the communist bloc, and hadn't mentioned the gold. So it was behaving dishonestly. The other country, which came later, did mention the gold, so was honest. Which country was it? He'd forgotten. The main point was the trucks running along rails, endless black trucks. With the hidden gleam of gold in their loads.

The synopsis looked as if it had been broken off. He was about to kick himself, but remembered that this was how he preferred his summaries. He was convinced that only in this way, with brief, vague, mysterious phrases, would they keep their suggestive power.

His eyes slid over his old handwriting, and he felt a first spark strike from his brain. Then another. Gold among the copper. A pale radiance, smothered by the mineral darkness. A secret message found somewhere deep down.

He could almost hear the murmur of his working brain. But the sparks were weak, and growing paler. They were almost extinguished. Oh no, he howled. Don't you leave me too.

Now he tried to think without their help. It was the question of which country would speak up about the gold. The second customer. It couldn't be the first one. Identity forgotten, it said in his notes. After the quarrel with the socialist camp, all the old contracts were torn up. The new customer, the honest country that had drawn attention to the gold, definitely mustn't be a Western state, but there were no friendly states left. After China, North Korea had gone too. That theatre delegation had been merely the latest effort to patch up relations with Cuba, of course in vain.

What the hell, he had to find some country that fitted the play, or rather his depression. He was no longer meeting Migena. They had both decided not to see each other, at least for a time. Albana's phone calls were petering out. Her internship in Austria had been extended again.

Some state, he thought numbly. He couldn't have the gold discovered by German or British Marxist–Leninists. Only Angola was left, although relations were very fragile after two snakes had got into the embassy building in Luanda and bitten the Albanian consul. It was said that the snakes were just a pretext, like in the story of that Trojan leader, and the real reason for the delicate relations was the presence of the Russians.

He thought of the map of the Soviet bloc, which always looked larger than it was. Endless wastes that expressed nothing. Leaving the bloc had brought neither exhilaration nor regret.

Automatically he went to his desk again, threw the ball of paper into the basket and took out a fresh sheet. *Bez slyoz, bez zhizni, bez lyubvi*. Without tears, without life, without love. Pushkin's cold line, as if straight from the icebox. *Act One. Scene One*, he wrote again. His right eye watched his writing hand in astonishment.

Ore Collection Point. Enter CZECH ADVISER.

CZECH ADVISER: Glory to labour, comrade.

ALBANIAN LABOURER: Morning, lad.

CZECH ADVISER: No good marning, that word mistake. Glory to labour. That's what say in Prague. Good marning forbeeden.

ALBANIAN LABOURER: Aye.

Rudian felt the last spark die. Nothing. Just slag. No gold, no divine spark anywhere.

Don't do this to me, he thought, without knowing whom he was addressing. He stood up, perplexed, and found himself next to the same part of his bookshelves where the meteorite had struck so many weeks ago between Scott Fitzgerald and *Toponyms*. A new place name should have been added to this book: the Rock of the Bride Killed by Lightning. Or simply, Black Rock.

It was here that he had hit her, at first without realising it. Only later did Migena mention, quite naturally, 'when you hit me there by the bookshelves'. After that he believed it too. When I hit you, my darling, that evening.

He had vowed it wouldn't happen again. But he reached out to rearrange the books so that at least Fitzgerald wouldn't be there if it did.

When I hit you, my darling, in front of a fellow writer. You lout, he said to himself. He had struck on the head the best girl in the world, heedless of the scandal, her protests, the possible X-ray.

For days he had been wandering round that dim world of X-rays of one sort or another.

He knew it was useless requesting Linda's breast scan. The hospital would say that her family had it. Her family would surely say that the investigators took it during the house search, with her diary, her few photographs, and of course the book with his dedication.

Explaining to the investigator would be the most difficult thing of all. It would be hard to persuade him that this was not a sentimental and still less a political matter. It simply had to do with his profession. Also, deep down, it was a health issue, as the psychiatrist had explained to him. Dealing with depression, blah blah blah . . . And it would be better not to mention the secret unifying thread between the gold that was intern—, or rather walled up, amongst the copper ore, and the vague outline on the breast scan. These were secret, inexpressible connections, like all the enigmas of art.

As before, he felt the spark die instantly, and he almost beat his brow against this same shelf, which try as he might he could not escape.

He pushed aside the books with his hand, rifling through them until he remembered that what he was looking for was not there but behind the complete works of Gorky. There was the little pre-war Beretta revolver that his cousin, an army officer, had found for him a long time ago. Whenever he thought of it he told himself to hide it in a different place, but it occurred to him that if they searched the apartment they would find it anyway, so he put it back where it had been, between volumes six and seven, Gorky's most optimistic works.

Was it the sight of the revolver that brought a slight and perhaps ironic smile to his face? He had often smiled at the memory of how he used to imagine the most suitable age to die. The literary circle at high school thought of nothing else. They all agreed that the most stylish age of death for a poet was before thirty. This was why they worshipped Lermontov. They should have rated Pushkin above him for quality, but Lermontov was ten years younger than Pushkin when he died in his duel, and therefore had the prior claim.

How crazy he'd been. He had really believed that after thirty, people would secretly turn their backs on Lermontov and attach themselves to Pushkin. How misguided we were, these people would say. We were young, what could you expect? Now Shakespeare's funereal forties lay ahead of him, and beyond them the loneliness of fame, with chandeliers and cold women who were more intimate with death than with you.

So there it is, he thought, finding himself back at his desk and staring at the blank pages in panic. You are a bit of a bully. It was Migena who had first said this to him, immediately after making love, qualifying what she said with a thousand apologies: excuse me, let me tell you something, don't take it the wrong way, but on the contrary, in all kindness, etc., etc. He had stopped her mouth with his hand so that she would not repeat 'I'm sorry', until finally he had pacified her, saying, I know, perhaps it's all that's left of my youth.

Act One. Scene One. The Ore Depot. Enter FOREIGN ADVISER.

The script was hopelessly tedious until the moment when one of the characters sang quietly under his breath, before the Polish or Mongolian adviser came on stage. Rudian had written the text of this song at the very beginning, when the idea of the play had flashed into his mind. He leafed through the pages, searching for it. Recently, whenever he was looking for something he became obsessed with the idea that it was lost. His temples thumped. His anxiety at having lost it was strangely mixed with another, deeper suspicion that he had not actually written the song but only imagined it.

Here it was at last. It was called simply 'Song', with no other title. He waited to calm down before he read it.

If death comes looking out for me
He won't discover where I'll be.

Don't be surprised, don't stand and stare
If I'm not here nor anywhere.

Don't explain and never weep.
This is a different death, another sleep.

He remembered well the morning when he had written these lines. After the line 'This is a different death, another sleep' he'd thought: Fantastic! He was sure that he'd discovered something entirely new, the sort of thing that happened once in a hundred or two hundred years: a different kind of death, something between a newly discovered continent and a new essence or system of mortality. But his elation was short-lived. He recalled the three domains of Dante, in any of which a fugitive might take shelter, and the excitement faded. And as the embers died down, so did the engine that was to drive the play forward. The trucks stood cold and black as before, full of ore that would yield nothing.

The trucks rumbled past in succession. After the thirteenth came the fourteenth, clickety-click, with the five-year plan overfulfilled, the pledges of the Fourth Plenum, the fifth quarter of the plan, clickety-click, and the half-extinguished gleam of gold in the depths.

Outside, the day was bleak. A taxi sped by in what seemed like simulated haste.

Black ore, he repeated to himself slowly, like a lullaby. Sleep, sleep, my little ore, my little black mineral.

The trucks rattled past on the iron rails. Nobody knew what their contents hid. *If my mother calls me home . . . Say I'm buried under black chrome.*

He shouldn't have taken that second Valium shortly before dawn. It was this that must have done for him.

Valium secundum on the dies irae. Truckibus rattling past one after another. Horribilis planus maledictus, clickety-click, and a requiem for you.

Enough! He could not tell if he cried this out loud. He had no need to keep persevering. Now that a dead language had appeared on the stage, he had got the message. He wouldn't write anymore, ever. Quando Judex est venturus. That's enough. He didn't care what the verdict on him would be. Suicide on the pretext of creative sterility. Trrakkk. Nihil.

He stood up, went to the settee and lay down with his head on the arm. The outline of a dream, dimly seen during the night, struggled to reassert itself in his mind. This happened to him very rarely during the day. The sign *Drini Hotel* was unambiguous. Third floor, room 307, Linda had said. If you have a problem with the porter, say you are from the hospital.

The porter looked half-asleep. 'Third floor, room 307,' Rudian said. 'You're from Oncology?' asked the porter. Rudian nodded. He had come equipped with a signed book, a souvenir from the author, but it seemed this was unnecessary.

Linda stood waiting for him in a white nightgown. She was more beautiful than he had ever imagined. They embraced without a word and she took his hand in hers and laid it on her breasts. He didn't manage to say a word to her about Cerberus, whom he had lulled to sleep. 'Don't be frightened,' she said as she drew him to the bed. 'I'm not a virgin.'

She must have noticed astonishment in his eyes, because she added, 'It's the only thing I kept from Migena.'

They made love with a strange feeling of surprise, as if it happened in some other dimension that was not yet part of the everyday world. Afterwards, a vestige of astonishment in his expression led her to return to their conversation. She had lost her virginity to the man Rudian had imagined. How strange, he wanted to say – but she did not let him. It was true, they called him Mr Right-Off and he was the last person she would have wanted to do it with. But as so often, this was exactly what had happened.

'I know,' he interrupted. 'You did it . . .' (At the last moment, he succeeded in avoiding the phrase 'for me', which seemed to him so banal.) 'You did it . . . so that we could be here.'

'Perhaps,' she replied thoughtfully. 'Of course,' she added. 'That was the main reason.'

Although she did not say 'but', the word loomed above them, cold and ambiguous.

'Why else?' he asked in a faint voice.

It just happened. The opportunity arose. It was Rudian's mind that formed this reply, while Linda remained silent.

'Why else?' he said again. 'Was there another reason?'

Linda hesitated.

'Of course,' she said at last. 'Of course there was. He was the only person who came to my funeral.'

He listened in bewilderment. Was it possible to accept such things so lightly, and say them so naturally?

He felt the creases of his brow furrow. There was no logic to this, he wanted to say. How could something that could only be done when one is alive be caused by one's funeral? Linda, as if understanding his bewilderment, said something linguistically incomprehensible, but which conveyed, more or less, the idea that from now on she inhabited a different realm, one that obeyed different laws.

He remained spellbound. 'I thought so,' he murmured again and again, until she asked, 'What do you mean?' 'I'm surprised that the mysterious stranger at the funeral, who was the subject of all those rumours, turned out to be him.' 'Why be so surprised?' she said. 'You knew that.' He became even more confused. 'Of course I found out later, like everyone else. But still . . .' he said. 'What do you mean, but still?' There was still a mystery. 'In the changing room, by the volleyball court, you didn't just give him a sign, as you told Migena, you pulled him after you.'

'Are you going to reproach me for that?' 'Not at all,' he said. 'I don't have the right to. I couldn't do that even if I wanted to.'

She put her fingers to his mouth. Then she took his hand and laid it again on her breasts. 'It was only something . . . what you might call . . . clinical. You know as well as I do. You're the first person really to kiss me,' she whispered. 'The first man, do you understand? And the first and last to touch me, or rather to trans-touch me . . . isn't that enough for you?'

Of course, he thought. To ask for more would be a sin.

She continued to murmur about the hand of fate, which had so arranged matters that the two of them, Linda and Migena, had gone with these two men, only to come together at that fatal moment which was the inevitable end of all that had been set in motion. As she talked, her words became vaguer, and some of them even seemed to be his own rather than hers. Her soul was evidently preparing to enter another dimension. She talked on about that divine coincidence, and the fatal moment when her breasts were touched at the dance by the wrong hand, and when the two men, Mr Right-Off and the playwright, the base and the noble, were to contest each other, like in the story of Barabbas and Christ.

The girl described rather more clearly the criminal investigation of Mr Right-Off, and the investigators' possible efforts to understand the riddle of why she had surrendered to him. They would find out everything else but they would never find the answer to this enigma, which would remain a secret known only to Rudian, and to Linda, who had taken it with her. She repeated the word 'never' and he wanted to ask how she could know about the investigation, because she was no longer of this world, but he remembered that his mind was now working for both of them.

They were gradually merging together in every respect, even sharing in that other realm. He had heard about this realm long ago, had even heard its anthem: *If you take me . . . You'll take a star, but not a wife.* He remembered hearing the song that dark night near the filthy beer hall – so similar to the one owned by the English widow Eleanor Bull – where he might be stabbed with a knife in some ruffians' quarrel, like that other playwright centuries before.

He told her about the song, although he could hardly remember the words.

It was about a girl who spoke of marriage, and even asks if the phrase 'the marriage crown' is still used, like long ago. It was a song almost dedicated to Linda.

Before he managed to tell her that she was not only unnatural, but non-existent, she asked him, 'Are you still suspicious? Are you rejecting me?'

He replied that he had no right to be suspicious, still less to reject her.

In fact it was she who was rejecting him.

He thought that she cried no in a resounding voice. That would be more than cruel. It would be unthinkable.

The girl suddenly looked distant. 'It was so difficult to come to you,' she said calmly. 'Impossible, really. Barbed wire stretching everywhere, so many dogs, and such cold.'

You don't understand, he almost shouted. It wasn't a question of suspicion or not. It wasn't up to him to decide. It was her decision alone. In this case, she was in a superior position. In front of her, everybody was guilty: this country, the times they lived in, everyone, including himself.

'I don't want anyone's pity,' the girl said. 'Or recompense.'

He thought it would take years to say all the things he had in mind. He was preparing to tell just the gist of it, that this cold, lifeless union was a violation of the order of nature. But to his own astonishment, instead of uttering these words – if fact in contradiction of them – he lowered his head as a sign of acceptance.

The girl seemed calmer, but without joy. She still shone coldly, and asked him again about the song. Wasn't it, after all, about marriage?

Suddenly, but still vague, the words came back to him:

> *Be careful, if you take me in this life*
> *You'll take a star, but not a wife.*

She stared at him, as if meeting the very centre of his own gaze. Then she asked, 'Are you scared of me?'

'No,' he said. 'Not of anything. I only have one fear, of losing you.'

And at that point he woke up.

THE SAME TIME, THAT SAME MORNING. IN THE LEADER'S OFFICE

His elderly secretary, after summarising the previous day's events and reading out the membership of a commission to draw up proposals for the next Central Committee plenum, continued with an even briefer report on the economic and cultural situation.

The Leader listened in silence. Recently, his interventions had been much less frequent. That morning, his secretary had expected he would interrupt to enquire about the state of health of Albania's consul-in-chief in Angola, following the snakebite. Or perhaps later, under the heading of culture, where the main subject was the publication in Switzerland of a French translation of the Leader's selected works. But he had been indifferent to both these things.

Energy situation. Mining industry. The secretary lowered his voice still further but, as had happened already two or three times, the Leader made a sign for him to stop where he least expected it.

The question concerned copper, or rather the gold that had been found in it two months before. Or still more precisely, any rumours following its deposit in 'the Party's fund' in Switzerland.

'There have been no rumours.' The secretary knew this wasn't the case, but still he replied calmly.

The sparkle in the Leader's eyes, that brief light that the secretary knew so well whenever an idea struck him, was instantly extinguished.

The gold in Switzerland had joined three or four other taboo subjects, the most important being a very private matter relating to his own youth which, at the insistence of his wife, the secretary had decided to conceal from him, in order 'not to cause him anxiety'.

The secretary had expected the Leader's attention to be roused by the events in the town of Gramsh, about which he had drafted a second report, more comprehensive than last month's. The Leader's eyes sharpened, especially when prison sentences were mentioned. These were graded, from the director of the school down to the musicians in the band, including the saxophonist who was the main instigator of the debauchery and, it was thought, would be sentenced to twelve years' imprisonment under Article 55. The case of the gym teacher was still under secret investigation. Besides being suspected of abusing his pupils, he was the only person apart from her parents who had gone to the girl's funeral, and in disguise too.

'You see, you see,' the Leader said.

The secretary paused in his reading, until the Leader prompted him. 'Go on.'

As for the writer Rudian Stefa, who was in a way the start of the whole affair, his case was linked to the in-depth examination of the girl's diary, and other issues that went beyond the framework of this report, such as his play, which had been shelved, and another play that was under consideration.

The secretary had raised his voice, certain that the Leader was following him with interest. He lifted his head from the text to say that he had received a very strange report from the psychiatrist Dr Z. regarding the playwright R.S.

'Really?' The Leader perked up. For the first time his eyes shone with delight. 'Ah yes, it's Doctors' Day today.'

Once a month, for more than ten years, special reports from the eminent psychiatrist had come directly to his office.

The report essentially contained observations on the psychic disturbances of people he had been treating for years. They were very high-level officials, sometimes from the Leader's most intimate circle, and people of distinction, writers and academicians. The secretary was sure that the Leader drew more sophisticated conclusions from his analysis of these reports, and especially of the nightmares described in them, than from the communiqués of the secret services. For instance it would have been almost impossible to expose the most recent conspiracy – in the oil industry – if the ringleader's sister-in-law hadn't visited the psychiatrist. She had revealed that the family of one of the oldest members of the Politburo lived in fear of their lives, and this was sufficient to unravel the thread. The secretary had never understood which group was in more danger, those who lived in fear because of their unquiet consciences, or those who didn't.

'Let's hear what the doctor has to say to us,' said the Leader, straightening his back. 'But let's have a coffee first.'

This was one of the secretary's favourite moments.

The Leader slowly sipped his coffee. The secretary as always could not decide which was better: to finish his coffee at the same time, a little earlier, or a little later. He went ahead and finished it.

In a steady voice he read the report on the depression of the young wife of the army's newly appointed chief of staff. It was hoped that her second consultation would shed further light on its causes. The two nightmares of the interior minister's mother-in-law could be of purely personal significance, but the finance minister's insomnia, now entering its second week, certainly was not.

'Aha!' exclaimed the Leader.

The secretary instinctively gathered his breath before saying the name of Rudian Stefa. The playwright was showing the first signs of madness.

The Leader had not looked so surprised for some time. The psychiatrist provided detailed explanations, as if he had long foreseen such a thing. Rudian Stefa's first symptom of mental derangement was his question, a while ago, of whether any country permitted engagement (meaning, in fact, marriage) with a dead person.

'Just listen to that!' the Leader said. 'How disgraceful!'

'There have been no symptoms of necrophilia,' the secretary continued. 'It's something else.'

'Something else,' the Leader murmured. 'That's easy to say, but just find that something else in a madman's mind. Go on, but skip those Latin medical terms.'

The secretary continued, but the Leader butted in again. 'Doesn't he say anything about what happened in Gramsh? As far as I remember, this playwright was mixed up in the affair. That girl who killed herself, an inscribed book, and I don't know what else.'

'No,' the secretary said. 'The doctor doesn't mention those things.'

'I see. He's a clever man. That's why I like him. He's impartial. He doesn't get mixed up in other people's business. If our boys in the Security Service knew this they'd have a field day. Writer looking for dead bride. Decadence in Gramsh. Agitation and propaganda to allow the living to marry the dead. The doctor doesn't comment on those things. That's all I know, he says, you deal with the rest. By the way, have they started a file on that writer?'

The secretary leafed through his documents.

'It seems they did initially, in the first flurry of the investigation. Then, for the reasons we know, they closed it.

'I see. Did anything come out of it?' the Leader asked. 'I mean, from that first flurry, as you put it?'

The secretary no longer felt on sure ground. 'Some conversations,' he said. 'Not very clear. More like gibberish. It seems the recordings were not very good.'

'Read out the transcript,' the Leader said. 'I like to hear them just as they are.'

'Maybe . . .'

'No maybes. Read them to me.'

The secretary obeyed. He had seldom felt more awkward. 'The seals are somewhere else noise from the street seven hundred years of solitude oh car horn don't say it Dante's farewell ball ah she loved you.'

The secretary looked up to see if he should continue. The Leader's expression seemed unconcerned.

'This raw data goes on,' he said. The Leader gave no sign of whether he wanted to hear more or not.

'They're talking about Dante's solitude,' he said quietly. 'Who knows who else's. I don't know what they are saying about mine.'

The secretary lost the thread completely.

He continued after this silence, hoping that at long last he would be told to stop. 'Courier of death.' The text became more macabre. 'The ghost no longer obeys me. I can't find the reason.'

Instead of telling him to stop, the Leader said, 'What is this ball, that's turned up for the second time?' The secretary felt a wave of self-pity.

There was no end to this horror. In fact, the gibberish unexpectedly petered out, but he still felt sorry for himself. There was an accompanying document from the Interior Ministry, asking permission to recruit as an informer Rudian S.'s girlfriend – and apparently wife-to-be, now on an internship in Austria – for the purpose, according to the Leader's well-known principle, of protecting the playwright.

Halfway through this long document, he raised his eyes to seek instructions, but the Leader's expression told him he was not listening. He wore the same look of surprise as when he had first heard the playwright's name, but it was now accompanied by a sad smile.

'We live and learn,' he said thoughtfully. 'I remember that in Gjirokastra they used to tell a lot of stories about searching for brides.'

Recently he had been thinking more and more often about the city of his birth. 'All sorts of stories,' he repeated, as if talking to himself. 'But never like this.'

He stood up slowly. It was time for lunch. The secretary escorted him to the anteroom, where the guards were expecting him, and returned to the office.

THE SAME MORNING. IN THE OFFICE, WITHOUT
THE LEADER

As always after the Leader had left, the office looked different and empty. From the files piled on the desk, the secretary opened the one on Gramsh and leafed through it for a while, without any clear idea of what he was searching for. Then he realised that the part about the gym teacher had a furtive attraction for him. The material was not fully organised and there were a lot of question marks and guesses, but perhaps here lay its appeal. Clearly the teacher had abused several students, and finally 'the girl'. That was how the file referred to her throughout, without giving her name. The investigation hadn't so far found any connection to the playwright Rudian Stefa, and still less to circles of royalist émigrés. There were unproven suspicions that the gym teacher had helped her to kill herself, and had found the poison for her, or had killed her himself to conceal something.

A second, more detailed investigation had concentrated on two questions: first, why the girl had given herself to him, and second, why he had gone to her burial. Part of the interrogation transcript was attached to the file. 'You admitted yourself that the girl was indifferent to you. Why did she suddenly change her mind? What did you promise her?' 'Nothing.' 'How did you threaten her?' 'I didn't.' The questions had continued almost until dawn. 'What did she expect from you? What did she ask for in return? Why?' He replied, 'I don't know. I don't know anything.'

The part about the funeral was equally obscure. 'Why did you go to the burial? Moral support for a family convicted of political crimes? Opposition to the Party line on the class struggle?' 'No, no, not at all. Nothing of the sort occurred to me.' 'Then why? Explain everything again. From the start, not forgetting anything.'

Again he had explained the events, the same story as before except that now a few words were garbled because some of his teeth had been broken during the interrogation. 'As a teacher of the socialist young generation, how could you be tempted by a girl from a former bourgeois family?' Vague answer. 'Students' changing room. Next to the volleyball court. It was perhaps the way she looked at me, which I took as a sign.' Nothing else, no explanation. 'Of her own free will, of course. She was a virgin.'

The questions that followed were almost the same. 'Why then? You said yourself that after what happened the girl became indifferent again as before. Why was that? Which of you didn't keep a promise? Tell us the truth. Why did she give herself to you? What did she expect from you? Why did she become cold again?'

'I don't know. I understood nothing. Perhaps that's why I went to the funeral. To find out. Her hair fluttered in the wind. I understood nothing. I was crying.'

The transcript ended here. Below it someone had written a note: *Idiot! Let him rot in prison.* Another note had been added in a different hand: *Not in prison – in the mine at Memaliaj.* At the end was the word 'clown'.

The secretary took a deep breath and leafed through the file to find the place describing the girl's surrender.

As he read he imagined, like in a slow-motion film, the changing room in the gym next to the volleyball court, the girl turning her head to look at the gym teacher. His apprehensive approach, and her arm drawing him to her.

Something resembling an electrical shock shot through the core of his body. He closed the file, put it back where it had been next to the half-Albanian, half-Latin ramblings of Rudian Stefa, and stood dumbstruck.

A pang that he had not experienced for thirty years suddenly hit him, searing, disabling him without pity. Twice he reached out his hand, but it would not obey him, until at the third attempt he drew out the file. He opened it at the same place, at the girl's playful invitation, and again stood dazed.

That character was only an ordinary gym teacher; how could he himself fall into this trap?

He put the file back in its place, as if it had burned his fingers, but it was too late.

Thirty years in his service and this incredible thing had happened.

He knew where this train of thought would lead. They had overthrown this class for all eternity, cast these people into the abyss with all their jewels, their memories and their love affairs. They had been reduced to dusty mummies, or worse, mere scaly residues, and yet now, when least expected, a girl from this class, out of the depths, *de profundis*, had struck a fiery spark.

It was all right for a moonstruck playwright or an idiot of a teacher. But he had been here thirty years, drinking from the clear spring. How could that spark have set him aflame?

An old song from his birthplace stirred below the surface of his mind. It was sung about someone who instead of dying honourably in battle, came to a shameful death among the womenfolk.

The Leader and his wife arrived unannounced. Present were two members of the Politburo, the half-blind parliamentary speaker and his wife, three or four ministers, and the newly appointed chief of the army's general staff with his young bride.

The Leader raised his fedora in greeting and took his usual seat by the large fireplace. 'Tell the comrades to come closer, if they like,' he said to his wife. 'Let's have a little chat.'

'Are you here for the first time?' the grey-headed wife of the parliamentary speaker asked the wife of the chief of staff.

The young woman nodded.

The Leader, talking to her husband, smiled and glanced at her.

'What a strange look he has,' the young woman whispered.

'Everything about him is like that – different,' the other wife replied. 'He was eyeing you with great curiosity, I could see.'

The young woman blushed.

The conversation by the fireplace grew livelier, and the two women could whisper more easily.

'When he enters, the whole room lights up,' the old woman said. 'With my husband it's the opposite. When he comes in, a cloud forms. That's what I tell him sometimes.'

The two women, scared of bursting into laughter, put their hands to their mouths.

'He's in a good mood this evening,' said the old woman, looking towards the fireplace. 'You can tell.'

The Leader trained his eyes on those who were not talking. His glance fell again on the wife of the chief of staff.

'Beautiful women don't often come here,' the other woman whispered into her right ear.

The young woman blushed again.

'Now you look even more beautiful.'

Silence had fallen by the fireplace, and the Leader's voice could be heard clearly.

'He's talking about the intellectuals. There have been some problems recently, have you heard?'

The young woman shook her head.

'Well, these writers . . .' the parliamentary speaker said.

'It's in their nature,' the Leader replied. 'We do so much for them, but they're never satisfied. They're always so persnickety.'

'What's that dreadful word?' whispered the young woman. 'I've never heard it.'

'You're right. Nobody uses it anymore. Where we come from, it means fussy.'

'These words are scary,' the young woman whispered.

'They behave like this because you're too soft,' the parliamentary speaker interrupted. 'If it were up to me, they'd soon see what I'd do to them.'

'Hear that?' the old woman said. 'Didn't I tell you he's crazy?'

The Leader pretended not to be listening. The silence was now absolute and even his breathing was audible. His next words rang out:

'They've always been like that. Never content. One says his frontal brain cells have been damaged, another complains that a ghost won't obey him.'

General laughter drowned his last words.

'Perhaps they're waiting for me to quit the stage,' he said slowly when calm returned. 'They think they'll have an easier time . . .'

The parliamentary speaker's dim eyes sparkled behind his black spectacles.

'Don't even think of such a thing,' the old woman called from where she sat.

The Leader gestured for silence, and then spoke.

'One who has turned up recently – I won't say his name, because I respect him – do you know what he wants? You'll never guess in a hundred years . . . dead brides.'

He paused and watched their eyes widen.

'You heard right. That's precisely what he wants, dead brides. *Sponsa mortua*, they would be in Latin.'

The company's ill-concealed mirth broke out at last and he had to gesture again for silence.

'What can I do for him, you may ask. I can't bring him a bride from the next world. All I can do is send him to his bride.'

The parliamentary speaker, growing agitated in his seat, was making signs with his trigger finger, and the Leader saw him. 'I know what you're thinking. Let's kit him out for his wedding and send him to his bride. But no,' he said, furiously shaking his head. 'No, no, no. I stand up for writers, crazy as they are.'

'Who's that angel over there?' the grey-haired wife said.

The Leader's right eye, visible from where the two women were sitting, seemed larger, velvety, with the glint of a tear.

'Who's that angel?' the woman said again. 'It's a *meleq*.'

'What does that word mean?' the young wife asked in a weak voice. 'You scared me.'

'It's an old Turkish word that nobody uses anymore . . . *Meleq*. The chief of angels . . .'

THE SAME EVENING. IN THE EMPTY THEATRE

The building was dark, as it was every evening, but Rudian Stefa thought he detected a faint light inside. He went through the yard to the porter's lodge by the stage door, and discerned the gleam of a cigarette and then the familiar silhouette of the caretaker.

He said good evening and asked if there was anybody in the theatre, or if his eyes had deceived him.

The porter replied that the plumbers were making repairs but he could go in if he liked. The side door was open.

Rudian was pleased that the staff remembered his old habit of sitting alone in the empty theatre on evenings when there was no performance.

He thanked the porter and went in. He sat as usual in the middle of the stalls between rows nine and thirteen, looking towards the stage. This had first been his whim, then a mania, and latterly the sign of a creative block, although nobody mentioned that. He himself offered no explanation. It just felt good. He could imagine the cherry-coloured curtain as the dress of an outraged woman, but offended by whom or what he could not tell.

The seats were the same cherry colour, as was the velvet in the boxes, including the state box.

He had not written many plays, but before setting them down on paper he had conceived them here as he sat in the empty auditorium, looking towards the stage.

There was a flight of steps on either side of the stage, less well lit than the stage itself. Usually they went unnoticed, but when illuminated by the pale lights at the sides, the audience knew that the actors would enter by them. These actors generally played the negative characters that populated the vast tracts of socialist realism from Berlin to Shanghai. They crept apprehensively out of cellars, air-raid shelters, debauched nightclubs, or hell itself. Suspicious plumbers, NATO spies, conspirators exposed at the Eighth Plenum, the Eleventh, or even the Second Plenum, which many people were convinced had never taken place at all, made their wretched appearances. They were followed shortly by Catholic priests, hoodlums with their molls, even the anxious shade of King Zog.

Rudian thought that these steps would serve him better than the stage. If destiny were still with him, of course.

The spot-lit pools wavered as if stirred by an invisible breath. 'Come, blessed spirit,' he murmured to himself, for some reason in archaic Albanian.

A shadow climbed the steps, visible before the figure itself emerged, the very character whom Rudian had been expecting. He carried an antique lyre with two new strings clearly distinguishable as a later addition.

Rudian held his breath, watching for what would happen. Would his beloved appear after him, or would there be no Eurydice?

We contrive our own great losses, he thought. But at that moment, a few paces behind the man with the modified lyre, the girl appeared. She stepped aside to avoid the body of the sleeping Cerberus, and then followed Orpheus with her head lowered, in the manner of Balkan brides.

Don't! Rudian cried inside. It was a famous 'don't', heard billions of times in human history. Don't turn your head, or you'll lose her.

'Orpheus,' the girl pleaded in a faint voice.

Rudian Stefa closed his eyes so as not to see what happened.

FIVE YEARS LATER. DAYTIME. THE OVERTHROW
OF THE STATUE

The roar from Skanderbeg Square came in waves. He opened a window but still couldn't tell in which direction they were dragging the statue.

The view of the square on the television screen remained the same. Amidst the confusion, you could see the truck on which the toppled bronze had been tied, but not the path they were trying to open up for its passage. The announcer was totally intoxicated and incapable of providing coherent commentary. He mentioned the theatre – 'It's heading towards the theatre' – but then cried, 'No, they can't get through that way. Oh God, this is incredible. The Leader, the dictator, trampled under the feet of the crowd.'

A change in the crowd's roaring made Rudian open the window again. The truck had turned into Dibra Street, as he had hoped. You could see people running alongside it on both pavements but not those who had climbed on top, who were visible only on the television screen.

Rudian put on his heavy overcoat and wrapped his scarf round his neck. The roar grew ever more deafening.

The truck came nearer. You could see the statue's legs and a part of its trunk. One of the people on top, with a lit cigarette, laughed for the cameras. Another appeared to be hitting the statue's jaw.

What, meanwhile, was the body deep in the earth doing, Rudian Stefa thought, as its image was desecrated?

The truck was almost below his windows. Soon the head would appear, cracked and dented.

The majority are under the earth, he thought, their bones broken, trickles of blood down their faces, and the poisoned cup in their hands. Explaining it to them would be the hardest of all.

The statue's head was directly below the window. The skull had split, and you could see the hollow interior.

'*Unreal mockery, hence,*' he said to himself.

The howls from the crowd below rose and fell.

The right eye of the bronze figure – huge, black and unnatural – seemed to be weeping.

THREE MONTHS LATER. LINDA B.

Of all the sounds above ground, almost none penetrated to the depths of the earth where Linda B. still rested in the corner of the cemetery in the little provincial town.

The Albanian regime was tottering but its laws remained in place, especially the regulations governing prisons and internment. One of these laws was extremely strange, and many people believed it must be unique to Albania. This law concerned political prisoners and internees who died before completing their sentences. Their bodies, even though vacated by their souls, had to continue serving their sentences in the grave, wherever they happened to be, until the end. Only after the expiry of the term of their sentence did their families have the right to exhume them from the cemeteries designated by the state, and take them wherever they wished.

The regulation, or rather the principle that the law applied identically below the ground as above, should have been the first to be revoked, but would apparently have to wait to be the last. The only persons not subject to this law were those who had served life imprisonment or had been shot. These two categories of prisoners were outside time, especially the limits of time in the legal sense.

Although prisoners and internees were subject to the same obligations on the basis of the same enforcement of the law above and below the earth, one distinction was made between them. All decisions regarding prisoners were applied individually, but because internment applied to entire families, decisions for releasing internees were also valid for their families as a whole.

Families generally consisted of many members, and some old people or infants would always die during the internment. So the famous 'directives' listed the names of the released family members in two separate columns: those in this world and those in the next.

The directive reached Linda B.'s parents not only five years to the day after its predecessor, but almost at the same hour, just before noon.

For the first time Linda B.'s parents took the envelope from the postman with indifference. Linda was no longer with them, and the directive had lost all meaning. They studied the state emblem on the envelope with dulled minds. What use was freedom now that they had lost their daughter? Furtively they even hoped the answer might be negative as before. Let them remain there in that backwater, where their daughter also lay.

But they felt they were committing a sin, and asked God to forgive them. Piously, they prayed again. It was not just because of their son that this feeling came, there was something more. 'What else could it be?' Linda's mother cried aloud. What else could it be but Linda?

She tried in vain to find peace. From deep down, obscurely, came an answer to her question. Of course it must be Linda. They could not leave, abandoning Linda there. With moist eyes, they tried to make sense of the directive that their son held in his hand: 'Her name is here, Mum, next to ours.'

After the initial shock, the meaning of what had happened grew clearer. They would not leave Linda. Indeed, their move, if they made it, would be more for her sake than their own.

Linda, under the earth, in the double shackles of the state and death, suffered more than her family above. If they couldn't free her from the chains of death, they could at least cut the heavier pair, the chains of the state.

They spent that whole unforgettable week dealing with documents. Linda's were more complicated, from the exhumation permit to be issued by the municipality down to the final certificate from the Interior Ministry, quite apart from the medical records. They wandered from one office to the next and often found themselves visiting the grave. The girl seemed impatient, so her mother would whisper the same words: 'Just a bit longer, my dear.' All four of them would leave soon, as if setting off for the cinema or a Sunday picnic.

Distant cousins in Tirana informed them that they had found a plot in the capital's western cemetery, outside the city in the direction of the sea.

They finally left one day in late May, all four in a small van. Three of them sat in the sideways seats, with Linda's narrow coffin between them.

It was a fine day with a gentle breeze. They had fixed Linda's hairgrip to the coffin as its only decoration. She had not taken it off after the farewell ball and they had found it in the mud outside the school.

Road signs announced where villages and towns began and ended. The van left them behind. Albania seemed extraordinarily big.

They craned their heads to read the first signs with unfamiliar names – *Motel Europa, Café Bar Atlantic* – to find out if they had now left the internment zone.

There was no sign anywhere to tell them this. 'I don't think there ever was,' Linda's mother said faintly. Her father said nothing, but her brother read the signs out loud: 'Café Vienna . . . Two Queens Hotel . . .'

The noise of the van's engine suddenly changed. The road ran uphill, but not steeply enough for the motor to gasp like this and emit such skeins of black smoke. The van barely moved, and the husband and wife studied again the landscape on either side, this time their faces pale with fear.

They didn't speak but later admitted to each other they had all sensed at the same time that the internment zone ended there, and the mute earth, in whose depths news arrived late, did not want to let their daughter's body leave.

The van recovered its normal speed. There was still the same May freshness, and Albania now seemed endless. They stopped a couple of times at small roadside cafés and ate and drank something with the driver. Linda's mother tried not to draw attention to herself, but glanced anxiously at the van parked to one side by the entrance.

Late in the afternoon they passed Durrës beach with its many villas and tourist hotels, their dance floors still empty.

The capital city showed signs of its approach, yet seemed further away than ever. Numbly they watched the telephone poles receding behind them, and looked at the farms and the helicopters in the small military airfields. Dusk was falling. Linda's father and brother surreptitiously observed her mother's cheeks. She had coped better than they had expected. It was only when the lights of Tirana appeared in the distance that first her shoulders and then her entire body shook with sobbing until she leaned forward and collapsed, huddled over the coffin. Amidst her sobs she spoke Linda's name, and sometimes, barely able to form the words, 'My daughter, my daughter.'

With the roar of applause ringing in his ears, he sat down in the chair where after premieres writers would usually autograph copies of their new play. The table was the same as in previous years, with its cherry-coloured baize, vase of flowers and glass of water.

He signed books according to the familiar ritual, rather wearily, cool with everyone, whether strangers or acquaintances. *A souvenir from Rudian Stefa*, or *With best wishes from R. St.*

There was also a covert ritual to the queue. People wore a special smile, as if passed on loan from one person to the next. Acquaintances who were uncertain if Rudian would remember them made sure he did. Some asked for a dedication with their name. Some were celebrities. Llukan Herri, above all. Colleagues, of course. One friend visiting from Germany, another from Canada. Foreign diplomats. Journalists. Migena holding her fiancé's hand. Both of them worked for the private television station Plus Channel. Most stood in silence, among them the investigator, whom Rudian had not seen for years.

The endless queue was exhausting.

A sweet voice said for the second time, 'Can you inscribe it with my name?' 'Of course,' he replied. Before he raised his head the unknown girl said her name: 'Linda B.'

Don't.

There was only this exclamation inside him, nothing else.

The impulse to raise his head was immediately supplanted by its opposite: a heavy chain weighing it down.

Don't, he said to himself again, but still without a clear reason. Don't look at her.

An irresistible longing, like an ocean of molten wax, enough to cover one half of the planet, flooded his entire body. And at the same time, the reason fought through a mist to make itself clear. Don't, if you don't want to lose her.

The book was in front of him and his hand began the inscription with awkward stiffness: *For Linda B., a souvenir from the author.*

Don't, he said to himself for the last time. However intense your longing and your desire, don't do it.

The order against making that old mistake was still in force. He obeyed.

As if blind, he raised the book with one hand while keeping his head lowered. He waited for her to reach for the book. The girl took it in her hand and just for a moment their cold fingers touched in that dark void.

Mali i Robit–Paris
Summer–winter, 2008–2009